Tennessee Plates

Claire Applewhite

Smoking Gun Publishing, LLC
St. Louis, MO

Cover and Interior Design by Smoking Gun Publishing, LLC

ISBN: 978-1-940586-07-6

Library of Congress Control Number: 2014915941

Visit us on the web at www.smokinggunpublishing.com

Published by Smoking Gun Publishing, LLC
Printed in the United States of America

Second Edition: September 2014

Acknowledgements

Each day, I appreciate the talented people in my life. Their feedback is as valuable as their ingenuity. Their creativity affirms my faith in the Muse.

To my husband, Tom: Your encouragement and support sustain me when energy and time run low. Thank you for your flawless proof-reading. Because of you, everyone uses the right gun, and the characters live, (and die), as intended. Bravo!

My sincere thanks to Lois Mans, my publicist and graphic artist, for her talent, support and friendship that continue to help me make a dream come true.

To the gracious people of Memphis, Tennessee: You're always in my heart.

Claire Applewhite
September, 2014

Dedication

For "Daddy"
Thomas Beasley Applewhite

Just yesterday, I thought of you,
while roaming through a store.
Chocolate, coffee, peppers, beer,
and condiments galore.

How you loved to tell a tale,
Your voice so full of zest.
It didn't matter what you said.
Your stories were the best.

I'm grateful for your counsel;
You found the time to spend.
You shared the things you learned with me,
told jokes, and were my friend.

I miss those times, and most of all,
I miss what I can't see,
The smile that told me I was with
that man from Tennessee.

Claire Applewhite
September, 2014

One

El Gallo Loco
Baños de Mujeres
Tijuana, Mexico
2:35 a.m.

Shelby knew the voices. Each night in the darkness, they whispered, *"Dinero, por favor."* The blade of *el cuchillo* caressed her throat while their soft, mean words pierced her soul.

A gunshot followed the scream. Shelby heard them call that name, the one they gave her the first night.

"Kimmy! *Donde está la rubia*? Kimmy Cruz!"

Through the open window above the sink, the darkness waited. *Could she squeeze through it?* The stench of sweat, grease, and stale beer swirled in the dusty air. Bile rose in her throat. She gagged, choked and swallowed; swallowed and choked. A single sound would expose her.

The footsteps grew louder, closer.

"Kimmy! *Donde estas*? *Dinero*, Kimmy! *Donde estas*?"

Alone in the moonlight, her trembling fingers grasped the slick porcelain sink. Inch by inch, they gripped and clutched at the ledge below the window. A lone cockroach scurried over the crackled tiles.

The rusty doorknob rattled behind her. *"Abre la pinche puerta!"* Gunshots shattered the flimsy door.

Scraped and scratched, Shelby clawed her way into the darkness. She had no choice. Like all the other times, she ran.

1

Two months later—St. Louis, Missouri

Shelby nestled into the tired mattress and pressed the receiver to her ear. Like hot fudge on French vanilla, his voice melted her soul. "Hey, Myles... Yeah, I was sleeping...I don't know. Ask me." She giggled. "Maybe. But, I sing tonight, you know that."

She fumbled on the nightstand for her cigarettes. She couldn't think without one or two or... All she knew was, when her ex-husband called, she wanted to talk. "Yeah baby, that sounds good. Oh, and Myles...by the way, my sweet man—I need another loan." She sucked on the cigarette and inhaled, staring at the cracks in the ceiling. "Aw c'mon, sugar. You know I'll pay you back, so if that's what... Yeah, I know Dr. Morton. I like him. A lot. What do you mean? Yeah, I said a lot. Like it's any of your business."

"Look, if you don't want to do his pre–nup, just tell him. Dr. Morton asked me if I knew a good lawyer, and of course, I know you, and... Look, don't blame me if the marriage blows up. I don't have a crystal ball. How do I know if they're going to make it? I've never even met his fiancé. In fact, I don't know the first thing about her. Nope. Not one little thing."

She swung her long legs over the edge of the bed and padded into the kitchen. Her black silk kimono clung to the curves of her body. When she spoke, a cigarette bobbed from the corner of her mouth. "If you want to see me, come by the lounge tonight—Maurice's place—you know, the club over on Greer. "Look Myles, I just need a few thousand. That's it. My break is around ten o'clock, and my dressing room is next to the kitchen. If I'm not there, I'm at the bar 'cause somebody nice bought me a drink." She stubbed out the cigarette and sighed. "Yes, I said the kitchen. Baby, I am not Barbra Streisand. Tonight, I am Krystal Light, take her or leave her. Yeah. Me too. Bye."

The Grapevine Detective Agency
6:45 a.m.

Elvin Suggs never thought this day would come. That was before 'Nam, and his wife's murder. The letter in his hand changed everything. At the sound of footsteps, he glanced up and saw one of his partners. Dimond "Di" Redding, a tall, fiftyish woman with copper hair appeared in the doorway of the kitchen. Vibrant and assertive, she was the widow of Don Redding, a former Green Beret and Elvin's best friend. When Elvin's wife Cherie left him, he decided to visit Di in St. Louis—and stayed.

"Morning, Di." He stood at the kitchen sink, his shoulders slumped.

"Elvin, what's wrong? You were so quiet in here I didn't know you were awake. Where's your dog?"

Elvin stared at the envelope. "She's outside."

"You going to tell me what's wrong?"

He sighed and took a deep breath. He waved the letter in the air. "It's just stuff I got to let go of. Nobody but me can do it."

Di approached him. "May I see that?" She nodded at the letter in his hand. Elvin placed it in hers.

"Shore 'nuf."

"This letter is from a guy that wants to buy your house. That's good news. You've had it up for sale for almost two years, haven't you? Since Cherie…" At the sight of Elvin's tears, Di bit her lip. "I'm sorry, El." She laid the letter on the kitchen table.

"Yeah, it's been about a year and a half since those Hubble brothers done killed my Cherie." He strode over to the table and once again, examined the letter. "I don't know. I guess I thought I might go back to Memphis, you know, someday."

"You did? I thought you planned to stay in St. Louis."

"I'm from Memphis, Di. It's what I know, and it knows me. I guess I always liked the idea that I could go back there, if I wanted to." He shook the letter in the air. "If I do this—if I sell my house—I can't ever go back. Not to that house, anyway. I'm going to have to think this one through. Take a little time."

Di didn't speak for a few seconds. When she did, her voice resonated with genuine curiosity. "I just don't get it. Why would you want to go back to the place where Cherie left you for another man?"

Elvin paused, and thought for a moment. Di's observation seemed to heighten his confusion. "I don't know," he said. "I really don't know."

Two

**Downtown St. Louis, outside of the Office of Parole and Probation
Later that afternoon**

When Ronald "Jupe" Jupiter spotted the two Mexicans, he felt like a dead man. His pace quickened. His pulse surged. Footsteps pattered behind him.

"Hey, Jupiter Ron!"

They remembered him! Well, he was packing heat. Once, when he was fifteen, he got caught without a pistol. *He never let that happen again.* He considered running away from them, but decided against it. No, he would confront them. Jupe stopped in the middle of the sidewalk and turned to face the two men, one tall and lean, the other short and pudgy.

"Yeah, what do you guys want? I don't have any money."

"Remember us?" Eduardo, the tall one, leered at him like a hungry shark. "St. Francis House?"

"The last time I saw you guys was in Texas." Jupe paused. "At the halfway house."

"The man has a good memory, Santy. Peanut butter and jelly, eh gringo?""

"Yeah. Right. But now, I don't have anything to say to you. I don't know much of what's going on around here. Haven't been around here long enough to know anything."

Eduardo glanced at Santy. Santy nodded and yanked a roll of bills from the depths of his pants pocket. "Maybe a little dinero can help you remember something to tell us, eh? Think, Jupiter Ron. Hard."

"What do you guys want? I told you. I'm busy."

Eduardo snickered. "He's busy. The man is busy!" He pointed at Jupe. "You are looking very skinny, Jupiter Ron. Not eating so good, eh? You could use some *dinero?* Maybe a steak? *Una cerveza fria?*

"What do you want?"

"The Kimmy. Where she go?"

"I don't know any Kimmy."

Eduardo snatched a photo from his wallet. "Ha! You know this girl? Think hard, Jupiter Ron."

"I'm thinking." He eyed the wad of cash in Santy's thick fingers. "How much is she worth to you?"

Eduardo's face brightened like a fresh daisy in the sun. "How much do you know?"

For a split second, the image of Shelby's face flashed into Jupe's brain, followed by the dingy jail cell in Texas. *What had she done for him lately?* Jupe chose his words carefully. "Tell you what, amigos." He watched Santy count the money, feeding the cash through his fingers like a deck of playing cards.

Eduardo and Santy stared at him with curiosity in their eyes.

"What you need is a contact."

Eduardo nodded. "*Sí*, a contact. That would be very good."

"Okay." Jupe lowered his voice. "You guys got a pen or something? Good. Write this down. The Galaxy on Grand Apartments."

"That is our contact?" Eduardo said.

"No. No. The contact is a person. But first, I need the cash. One thousand dollars." He extended his flattened palm. "Lay it on me."

"Pay him, Santy." Eduardo looked almost angry. "This contact is very good, Jupiter Ron, eh?"

"Rock solid, Eduardo." Jupe's mouth curled in a half–smile. "Air tight."

"Where you meet this contact?" Santy asked.

"Prison. Where else?"

Santy shrugged his meaty shoulders. "Of course." He counted the stack of C–notes into Jupe's hand. "Eight, nine hunred, one tousand."

"*Hokay*," Eduardo said. "Now, our contact, *por favor.*"

Jupe folded the bills and stuffed them into his thin wallet. "Are you ready? Write this name down. Nester Arseneaux. It isn't easy to spell, so I'll do it for you. Got it? Nester's the manager. He's a friend of mine. Tell you anything you need to know. Just don't push him too hard."

Eduardo grinned again. "Santy and I, we never push."

Santy did not smile. "Arturo will do that." Nevertheless, he patted his gun. "Have a good day, Jupiter Ron."

"*Si. Muchas gracias*, Jupiter Ron." Eduardo said. "We'll be in touch."

The Lounge by Maurice
10:30 p.m.

The place smelled like a wet dishrag. Perched on a bar stool, Shelby sipped a diet cola and winced. The tart tang lingered in her mouth. A smoky haze blurred the faces. *Where was Myles?* The back door cracked and closed, and a hunk of finesse appeared. *There. There he was.*

When Myles slithered into a room, women of all ages noticed him. Denzel mixed with Samuel L., his lips curled in a devilish grin; that easy smile telegraphed an edgy, irresistible allure.

"Shelby!" His lips grazed her fingertips. "My lady." A tailored suit draped his toned body. His tapered fingers sported a ring with an *M* encrusted with diamonds.

The blonde took a deep breath, and remembered the good times, because honey, with a man like Myles, there were just so many. Those were the kind of times that kept her coming back for more. "Talk fast, Myles. My break's almost over."

"You know I'm a fast talker, baby. I'm late 'cause I was looking for your dressing room. It was like you said, next to the kitchen. I asked Stockpot back there for directions, and did he ever laugh. What gives?"

"My dressing room is an old closet. Maurice lets me use it to change. It's a joke, but this place isn't my forever. Someday, I'll go back out West, maybe Vegas." She glanced at her rhinestone-studded watch. "What I need is a break. A big, fat break." She crossed her legs and sipped her soda. "Okay, you already know what I need from you." She laughed and flashed the half-smile she knew he loved. "Why do you want to talk to me? You getting married again?" Shelby leaned forward and stared in to Myles's eyes. "Tell me, baby. What's she like?"

Her ex leaned on the Formica table. His elbow nudged an ashtray. "Two divorces cured me." He chuckled. "I am not getting married again." He lowered his voice and glanced over his shoulder. "Shel, I need to know the truth about something." He cleared his throat. "Or, I should say, somebody." He shook his head. "This dude came into my office yesterday. He said you referred him."

"Did he dress like Dr. Morton?"

"Far from it. Not even close."

"What's his name?"

"I'll get to that in a minute. Now Shel, we have to have an understanding up front. Please, darling, don't refer people to me without asking me first. Cool?"

"Sure. What's up?"

"Looks like your dude is in a lot of trouble."

"I'm not sure who this guy is, but if he makes you so nervous, don't take his case. You won't hurt my feelings, baby."

"Oh, but there's a lot of money involved, and let's not forget, one of my favorite ex–wives needs a loan. I might decide I want to take his case."

"All right with me. But, if you're gonna be all up in my face all the time about a little cash…"

felt eerie. She couldn't explain it, but the feeling that someone was watching her all the time, well, it haunted her—she'd told Myles as much when he first brought her to The Galaxy to look at an apartment.

"No baby," Myles said, in his smooth, suave voice. "It'll be fine. I know other folks just love it here." Shelby hadn't met any of those clients yet, nor had she noticed the rows of doors painted the color of an orange inferno—until she signed a six-month lease. Somewhere, a television droned about sparkling dentures. *Hey, what was that odor?* Stale cigarette smoke, strong perfume…garlic, maybe onions.

She twisted the scratched doorknob, and once again, she shoved. "C'mon, open up," she whispered. It didn't budge. *Why did people paint cheap doors with ugly paint?*

Shelby's shoulder strained against the grainy wood. The door surrendered. She slammed it, and raced into the apartment. With her back pressed to the door, she gulped a breath of stale air. Maybe now, she could relax. She lit a cigarette and inhaled, blowing smoke into the still air.

A bitter stench filled the musty room. Moonlight streamed through the sliding door. Shelby started to walk across the room, and tripped. When she looked up, her gaze fixed on the tiny scarlet stains spattered on the yellow kitchen wall. When she looked down, she saw a limp heap.

Adrenaline sparked Shelby's fatigue; she opened her mouth to scream, but her voice seemed trapped deep in her throat. She gawked at the mound on the floor, still and silent. Despite the shadows, Shelby recognized the thick blond hair, tangled and matted beneath her favorite cowboy hat. *Claire Ireland.* They looked so much alike, people thought they were twins. The last time she'd seen Claire, they worked a show in Tijuana. After all they'd been through together, she'd know her anywhere. *How did she get here?*

The air reeked of garlic, onions, and cigarettes, and Shelby covered her nose with her hand. She stared at Claire's face, and her head throbbed. She didn't want to imagine all that happened before her arrival. Her trembling fingers started to dial Myles's number, and stopped. No one needed to know where she was headed for a while—maybe ever. With or without money, she needed to leave.

Shelby dropped the receiver. It tumbled onto the stained carpet beside Claire's ear. "If you'd like to make a call, please hang up," the recording droned.

Shelby rushed to the bedroom closet and rifled the pockets of her sable coat, the one Arturo gave her when she moved in with him three years ago. *Cash.* Her fingers probed the satin lined pockets for the five thousand dollars she'd stashed when she moved into the Galaxy Apartments two months ago. The pockets were empty. Someone beat her to it—someone who knew about the coat, someone who knew about the stash. *Arturo, or one of his men.*

Somewhere in the back of her mind, she knew this day would come. She just never thought it would come so soon. Shelby snatched the coat and her "bug out" bag—the one she kept packed in case she ever needed to leave in a hurry. Still, the question nagged at her. *How did they find her?*

Ten minutes later…

Shelby's foot mashed the accelerator, and the silver Caddy roared onto the highway. Gliding in the darkness, her heart pounding, she couldn't get the image of Claire's face out of her mind. Arturo ordered Claire's murder. Of that, she felt certain. The day that Shelby left, she knew there would be the payback, *La Restitucíon.* A sudden fear overwhelmed her. *Did Claire come to her apartment on her own? Or, had she been killed somewhere else and brought to her apartment? Was it a warning to the Kimmy? Or, did the murderers believe they killed Kimmy Cruz?*

She decided such speculation was futile. She also decided she needed to start another life somewhere, far away, this very minute, in a remote, offbeat place that Arturo's men would never find.

It wouldn't be long before Myles began to search for her. Not only did he know her schedule like the back of his hand, he had a nasty habit of turning up at the most inconvenient times. But, for now, she needed to forget about Myles and Jupe. She had bigger monkeys on her back, the ones that called her "The Kimmy."

A police car paused, and the red glare from a flashing light shined on her car. She glimpsed her face in the side mirror—gaunt, strained, worried. *Who was that woman?* She wished she could stop running long enough to find out.

For Shelby's money, the best getaway existed in Wisdom, Tennessee, at the El Dorado Trailer Park. No one would look there for her, or anyone else, because Wisdom wasn't on a map. Shelby's Mama discovered the place about ten or so years ago. She still lived there, though Shelby had to admit, she hadn't visited Mama for a couple of years. Hadn't exactly heard from her, either. She wondered if she still had that crazy boyfriend with the patent leather jumpsuits and the sunglasses. And she sure hoped she cut down on the cigarettes and Coca-Cola. Well, she reminded herself, she was in no position to dictate to anyone. Shelby smiled, and gunned the engine. She didn't plan to stop till she crossed the Tennessee state line.

St. Louis, Missouri, 7:45 a.m.

Elvin exhaled and rose from the floor. After a morning run and fifty pushups, he felt invigorated. His Airedale, Savannah, watched him with rapt admiration. "Hey, Vanna," Elvin said, "how 'bout you and me go get ourselves some breakfast before we hit the road?"

His gaze drifted to the crisp, white envelope on his dresser. "Times like this, Vanna, I do wish you could talk."

"What do you want to talk about?" Di stood in the doorway, and sipped coffee from an over–sized mug.

Elvin looked a bit embarrassed. "I don't know if I'm ready to say goodbye to my house yet."

"Even though you have a buyer?" She nodded at the envelope on the dresser. "I thought you were going to Memphis today."

For a moment, Elvin didn't speak. He pursed his lips and gazed at Vanna, then Di. "I am."

"Okay. I just thought you wanted to get an early start."

"Shore 'nuf. What time is it?"

"It's about ten minutes before eight o'clock."

"We'll be out of your way in a jiffy, won't we Vanna?"

"El, what's wrong? You're not acting like yourself."

Elvin flopped on the worn sofa. "I don't exactly know, Di. Guess it's just the idea of saying goodbye to that itty bitty house I bought with Cherie all those years back."

"I thought you said you wanted to wrap up your business in Memphis. You know, start over, move on."

"I did. I want to. It's just…I don't know. I wish I had better business to wrap up, that's all. I didn't do such a good job in the husband department, did I?"

Di didn't want to delve—again—into the tumultuous past that surrounded Elvin's divorce, much less Cherie's untimely murder. "Do you want me to go with you?"

"No. I'll be down and back in no time. C'mon, Vanna."

Di watched her old friend shuffle to his bedroom. His shoulders slumped. His feet dragged. "You sure you don't want any company?"

"Nope. Gotta do this one on my own."

"Okay." Still, she almost packed an overnight bag. At the thought of Cherie, her resentment surged. When that little blonde number lived, she caused Elvin more heartache than one man should ever have to endure; now, despite her demise, Cherie's memory continued to haunt him.

The sight of Elvin and Vanna disrupted her brooding.

"Okay Di, we're off," Elvin said.

"You know when you're going to be back, El?"

"Don't rightly know. It shouldn't take long, but…"

Myles grinned. "Yeah, that's right. I'm an attorney. I like to think I'm a good one."

"That's good, because I'm gonna need a good one. I pushed a few drugs back in Reno, okay? That's where I first met Shelby, and that's what landed me behind bars. And, by the way, if you ever meet Shelby Swain, don't go judging on her about a few drugs. She was in a very rough place after her divorce. I don't know that bastard ex–husband of hers, but I'd like to get my hands on him. Put him through a little bit of what she went through, you know?"

"Um, yeah. Understood. Please, go on."

"Yeah. Well. We had a little fight one day, you know how women can get sometimes. And she took off, headed for Missouri. At least, that's where she said she was going. You know, she used to have a gig somewhere around there on Saturday nights, and sometimes through the week on Thursdays—Thursday was All You Can Eat Rib night at the truckstop, just outside of St. Louis. Her stage name was Krystal Light."

Myles chuckled. "Cute, real cute. What did she do?"

"A little singing, dancing, whatever kept the crowd drinking. Hey, I don't know if you've ever been in some of those little towns in Missouri, around those parts, but it ain't Las Vegas."

"So I've been told."

"Yeah? You been to a few of those places, have you?"

"No, Mr. Jupiter, I haven't had the distinct pleasure—yet, anyway."

"Did you wonder why the Mexicans wanted to know where this Kimmy lady was, Mr. Jupiter?"

"Will you call me Jupe like everybody else? The Mr. Jupiter stuff is really getting on my nerves. No. To answer your question, I didn't. Because, for starters, I don't know any woman named Kimmy. Never did."

"Really?"

"Really." Jupe glared at Myles. "So that's all I know. I saw the front page with the picture of Shelby and heard a blonde was juked over

at the Galaxy on Grand last night. And I kinda feel bad about it—
wondered if it had anything to do with this Kimmy person."

"So, you read the newspaper, do you?"

Jupe chuckled. "Are you kidding me? It's all over the front page of
the St. Louis Post–Dispatch. Hey, don't look so surprised. I check out
a newspaper when I can get one, but it ain't like I got a subscription
or anything. I don't even have an address. Anyways, I'm good friends
with Arseneaux over at the Galaxy."

"Where did you meet Mr. Arseneaux?"

"Mr. Arseneaux, you calling him now? He would like that, he really
would. He's totally into respect. To answer your question Counselor,
we did a little hard time together, back in Texas. Don't look at me like
that. Hey, you know, Arseneaux's a very smart guy. Went to college
and everything. I think that's why he watches *Jeopardy* all the time."

"Right." Myles rose from his leather chair and extended his hand.
"Well, Jupe, I'll be in touch. I appreciate your candor."

"My what? Never mind, just save it. Look, Counselor, I don't
know what all a this means. Maybe nothing, like I said. But, I thought
it looked funny, and besides, if those Mexicans wanted me to keep my
mouth shut, they should have paid me better. You know?"

Better? Better than what? Myles shook his head. "Possibly."
He watched Jupe shuffle out of his office. He decided he didn't want
to know.

Four

The Primo Compound
Tijuana, Mexico, 9:00 a.m.

Arturo Primo faced the morning sun, and popped a juicy grape into his mouth. Three days passed since he ordered Eduardo Ruiz and Santos "Santy" Corejos to return the Kimmy to him. *And today? No Kimmy. He supposed he would have to take the matter into his own hands. No one would be happy if he had to do this, especially him.* As if it could sense Arturo's frustration, the telephone jangled on his massive desk. Arturo snatched it on the second ring.

"Hallo?" A broad smile spread across his tanned face. "Ah, Eduardo! What you say? You foun' her? The Kimmy? My money? My dinero, eh? Kimmy kill my baby brother, Hector, with his own gun, the thief."

"Say no more, Arturo. We found our contact."

"What you mean?" Like a beach ball on a flagpole, Arturo's bovine head seemed oddly balanced on his crinkled neck. When he grew excited, it wobbled from side to side. "Where you fine this contact? Answer me, Eduardo!"

"You remember the Jupe, eh?"

Arturo laughed. "Who wouldn't? I only wish there were more like him. He is working again, *sí*?"

"Hard to tell. He wouldn't say much. But, he give us a contact for the Kimmy. Of course, we had to pay him."

"Of course." Arturo's voice grew louder. "How does Jupe know the Kimmy?"

"He tell us he met her in a club in Reno. When she leave Tijuana, she go to work in Reno. Jupe say he was with her for a while. Then, she say she is going home."

"*Home? Where is home?*" Arturo pounded the table with his meaty fist. A crystal tumbler clattered to the floor, and shards of glass covered the terrazzo floor like a blanket. "This is her home!" He sighed. "Hokay. Where is she now?"

"That is the best part. The Jupe, one day he is talking to his fren in San Luis. His job is manager in aparmenn building. Guess who he rent aparmenn to?"

"Who?"

"The Kimmy, Arturo!"

"Only now, she when she works on the stage, she call herself Krystal Light."

Arturo guffawed like a hyena. His triple chins quivered like jelly. "*Krystal Light.* Ha! The woman has sense of humor. I like that. So, where is she now?"

Eduardo grew solemn. "Arturo, I have something to say."

"Eh? Speak up, Eduardo."

"We found Jupe's contact. We found the Galaxy on Grand Aparmenns, eh? We fine her aparmenn. And, we fine the money."

"*Dinero?*" Arturo said. "*Sí? Bueno! Quanto?*"

"Five thousand American dollars. In pockets of the sable coat."

"*Sí*, the coat. A present from me. Ungrateful thief. She must pay for this."

Eduardo's voice trembled. "We thought we got her, Arturo."

"Eduardo, you talk like an idiot. You foun this man, he foun the apartment, the sable coat, the money, and you don't got the Kimmy? What is wrong? What is it?""

"Arturo, Santy killed a woman. And, she is the wrong Kimmy."

"What are you talking about? Why you do this?"

"Santy kill Claire."

"Oh, my God…not my Clara." Arturo put his head in his hands

and wept. His body shook with grief.

"Arturo…"

"My Clara? How you make such a mistake? *How?*" He wailed like a wounded animal.

"Claire Ireland was in Kimmy's apartment. They look the same, Arturo. Our contact, he let her in the apartmenn before we get there. We think she went there to tell her we were coming, eh?"

Arturo stopped weeping. "You believe that, do you?"

"Yes, Arturo. I do."

"Then, good riddance."

"Can you fine him again? I want to talk to him."

"We can fine anybody. You know that."

"This man, can we truss him?"

"We don't know. He works for money."

Arturo grinned. "But, of course."

He stared out the window for a second. "This contact. I ask you again. Can he be trusted?"

"We know he is a very smart man."

"Hokay."

"We might have to kill him. After we get the Kimmy, of course."

"Hey."

"*Sí.* That is no problem."

Arturo grabbed a pen and his personal stationary. "His name?"

"Nester Arseneaux."

Again, Arturo chuckled. "Arseneaux, eh? I like it. Good work, Eduardo."

St. Louis, 10:00 a.m.

The two men shared their Hispanic descent, but there, the similarity ended. Beyond their heritage, they differed in every way possible. Take their taste in food, for example.

Eduardo, the tall one, spoke first. "What do you call those?" He pointed at his companion's plate, piled high with pancakes.

Santos, or Santy, as he liked to be called, smeared each one with peanut butter and grape jelly, then rolled and stuffed the melting purple mess into his wide mouth. It didn't seem that the burly man could eat the sticky peanut rolls fast enough to suit him. He shrugged with indifference. "I don't call it nothing. Why does it need a name?"

"Everything in America has a name."

"Jupiter Ron say peanut butter and jelly is for real Americanos. If a person no eat peanut butter and jelly, he say they must be an imposter." Santy lowered his voice and glanced around the room. "I put it on everything, Eduardo. You never know who is watching. *Sí?*"

Eduardo observed the bright purple jelly ooze from the ends of the pancake roll. "You have gone crazy, Santy. Why you want to be so American, eh? How can you forget Arturo's generosity to us? Have you become the Kimmy?"

"No," Santy said. "I never steal from Arturo."

Eduardo paused for a moment, and considered his next words. "That is good. Remember, Santy. Arturo never forgets the thief."

"The Kimmy?"

"*Sí.*"

"We don't forget her either." The tall man rose from his seat and straightened his tie. "We have much work to do."

The radio crackled, and Shelby fumbled with the buttons on the dashboard to find a clear channel. *Did she hear something about a tornado warning?* She studied the gray sky, tinged with violet and green. *Would Mama's trailer survive a tornado? Well sure. Mama and her trailer survived everything.*

A whirring sound, followed by a whine, hummed from the front of the car. *She knew she should have changed the oil. She probably should have replaced the spare tire, too. And there was that major overhaul on the transmission, but Leon at the shop wanted $568.00 to fix that, and that was rent money. Sometimes, a girl had to choose between tomorrow and today.*

The road sign said 100 miles to Memphis. If she could just make her way there, she'd be okay. Mama's friends knew people who knew people that would be glad to help her out. Memphis was like that.

Two hours later

The rain pelted the windshield of Elvin's car like a gushing waterfall. The oldies station played the Motown version of "My Girl," and Elvin sang along with every word. "Hear that, Vanna?" He sang about sunshine on a rainy day. "Used to be talking about my Cherie. Yeah." The Airedale blinked and stared at him with expectancy in her keen dark eyes, as if Cherie might appear any second. "No, gal. Don't get your hopes up. My little lady ain't coming back no more." Elvin laughed. "Didn't mean to get you all riled."

The rain eased a bit, though the radio announcer said a tornado touched down in Sikeston. "Maybe we should get a burger, Vanna. Yeah, I thought you'd like that idea." His eyes drifted to the side of the road. "Hey look, there's a car looks just like ours." He cracked his window, and peered into the driving rain. "Even got itself some Tennessee plates." He pulled over to the shoulder on the highway and stopped the car. "Looks like a lady's done broke down in the rain, shore 'nuf. You stay here, Vanna. No use getting you all wet, too."

***

She spotted him through sheets of rain. The mound of a man plodded through the deep puddles as if they didn't exist. For a moment, Shelby figured he was a cop, and she prepared to run. Then, she saw that Tennessee smile, broad and friendly. *He was from around here. Oh yeah, he was.* She'd bet her life on it, but she hoped she wouldn't have to bet her life on anything anymore. She'd already done enough of that to last the rest of whatever life she had left.

"Hey," she said.

"Hey, yourself." He extended his hand. "Name's Elvin. Elvin Suggs."

Shelby shook his wet hand. It felt warm. "Well, which is it?"

"Ma'am?"

"Is it Elvin or Elvin Suggs?"

The man grinned. "Kinda wet out here to be so particular, ain't it? I answer to either one, ma'am. You can just call me Elvin. That'll be fine. This your car?"

"Yeah. It is. Was, I mean. It died a few minutes ago, and I was fixing to call my mama."

"Your mama? Where's your mama's house? I could give you a ride, if it isn't too far from here."

Shelby knew he was going to say that. Of course he was going to say that. All men offered to take her someplace, sooner or later. But, she had a different feeling about this one. He seemed different from the rest.

"Okay. Where we headed?"

"You know the El Dorado Trailer Court in Wisdom?"

"No ma'am."

"Just outside of Memphis. By the Mississippi state line."

"Shore 'nuf know those parts. Ma'am, I don't mean to be forward or nothing, but if you don't mind, what's your name?"

"Shelby Swain." She smiled and looked away.

He opened the passenger side door to the Caddy. "Okay then, Shelby, now you get to meet the best part of this ride."

"We got company?"

"Oh, yeah. I forgot to tell you about Vanna."

"Another girl?"

"Well, I guess you could call her a girl, but she looks like a dog."

"Why Elvin, no matter what a girl looks like, you shouldn't call her a dog."

Elvin grinned at the fuzzy Airedale lounging in the corner of the backseat. "This is gonna work out just great, isn't it Vanna? Come on girl, slide on in!"

"So, it's Shelby, is it?" Elvin smiled a bit and glanced sideways at his passenger. The faint scent of Shelby's spicy perfume filled the air. "Vanna and me were going to grab a burger. How does that sound to you?"

Shelby turned to stare at the large terrier, sitting on the seat behind Elvin. "So, this is Vanna?"

"How'd you guess?"

"This car isn't that large, Mr. Suggs."

"Call me Elvin. Or Suggs. Just don't call me Mister anything."

"Fine. You know, I am a little hungry. It's been a while since I ate."

"How long you been on the road, Shelby?"

The blonde turned her head and Elvin sensed a stony silence. "Shelby? I said…"

"You asked me how long I've been on the road." Shelby stared out the window. "And, I'm thinking." A few moments lapsed before she spoke. "I heard you, Elvin."

"Shore 'nuf." Elvin stared straight ahead, but said nothing. *What did he say to offend this gal? Di would know, he felt certain. Di always knew what he did wrong.* Never thought he would miss that part of having Di around, but then, a man never could tell what he might miss about a woman. When he lost Cherie, that lesson became his reality. "Burger Barn okay by you?"

"I'm not picky."

Elvin grinned. "Well, we sure aren't, are we, Vanna?" The silver Caddy cruised onto the ramp. The terrier began to drool on Shelby's arm. The signature red structure with BURGER BARN in large white letters awaited them on the hilltop.

"Does Vicki eat hamburgers?" Shelby frowned and glanced at Vanna.

"Shore 'nuf. Mostly, we eat the same thing, see. I buy her dog food, sure, but Vanna likes what looks good. I can't say that I blame her. Besides that, she eats the dog food, too. Tell you what, her favorite is the Barn Buster—maybe you would like that too, you being a girl and all."

Shelby stared at Elvin for a second and then burst into laughter. "You've got to be kidding me."

"Well, it's a lot to eat. Maybe you're on a diet."

"No, that's not what I mean."

"You don't like mayo on your burger?"

"No, that's not what I mean."

"Well, then let's hear it, because I'm ready to order."

"I've never met anyone quite like you, Elvin Suggs."

Elvin shrugged. "The woman I live with says that all the time."

Shelby's expression changed, in a way that Elvin didn't quite understand. He wasn't certain, but he could have sworn she looked disappointed. Now that was crazy, he told himself. She didn't know him. He imagined it, that's what it was—his imagination. He would ignore it.

No, he wouldn't.

"Di's just a friend, now, Shelby. Don't misunderstand."

"You live with a woman who's 'just a friend?' C'mon Suggs, I was born at night—just not last night."

"Don't read you there, Shelby. Di's my friend. Cain't never be nothin' more than that."

"Why not?"

Elvin opened the car door and came around to the passenger side to help Shelby out of the Caddy. "Lots of reasons. Vanna, for one. Her husband's another."

"You live with a married woman?"

Elvin looked shocked. "No, ma'am. Di was married to Don, but he ain't with us no more. He was my best friend in 'Nam."

"So Di's a widow?"

"Shore 'nuf."

"So, she's available?"

"I guess she is. To somebody. She tried that a while back. Didn't work out, though."

"Why not?"

"Guy was crazy. Wanted to experiment on animals, do stuff with electric shock treatments and popcorn. He even wanted to experiment on Vanna."

"Maybe that's what your Di liked about him."

Elvin stopped walking and paused. "You know something, Shelby? You might be on to something there. I never thought about that. He seemed crazy, but maybe he wasn't." He paused again. "He sure acted crazy."

"What happened to him?"

"Cobra shot him."

"Who's Cobra?"

"Ma'am?"

"Cobra? Is that a person—or a snake?"

"Oh." Elvin chuckled. "He's a person, alright. Nervous kind of guy, but he gets by. He just feels a whole lot better with a gun in his hand. That might be hard for a lady like you to understand." Elvin sensed her hesitation, but he restrained his urge to deluge her with nosy questions. Di would have been proud. This habit required extraordinary "Suggs" effort.

"Your friend Cobra is a good shot, is he?" Elvin noticed that Shelby didn't even flinch at the mention of Cobra's gun. In fact, she seemed intrigued at his skill, a fact that intrigued Elvin.

"Yes ma'am, he is. Cobra was a sniper in 'Nam, Marine–brand kind of guy. Wishes he was back there, I do believe. He would tell you otherwise, but the man doesn't know what else to do with himself. Every chance he gets, he shoots something or somebody, I should say. But, that's a good thing, since we run a detective agency. Or did I already tell you that part?"

Shelby's eyes widened at the mention of his detective business. Elvin noticed that part. He also noticed her big blue eyes, and that wavy blond hair with the curls on the end. Pretty lady this Shelby Swain. Looked a lot like Cherie…

"No, you didn't."

"I didn't?" Elvin's reverie faded, and he found himself standing at the counter of Burger Barn.

"Your detective agency. You didn't say anything about it."

"Oh," Elvin said. He glanced down at the empty leash in his hand and panic pulsed through his veins. "Vanna! Where did she go?"

Shelby giggled. "You left Vicki in the car, remember? You said they don't allow dogs in here."

"I said that?" Elvin felt confused. He didn't recall saying that, or for that matter, anything else, even the way that Shelby called his dog "Vicki." This Shelby Swain made him forget mostly everything about the past and even the present. For the first time in a helluva long time, he felt a kind of magic he thought died a long time ago. He noticed other men in the Burger Barn staring at him with envy at his good fortune in earning a place at Shelby's side.

He couldn't believe he said anything about leaving Vanna in the car. *Had he really said that?* Well, a fresh, hot Barn Buster bought a lot of forgiveness. Vanna could tackle two all by herself, and Vicki, whoever she was, probably could too. The way he was going, he would flub up a lot more before they hit Wisdom, Tennessee. It was going to be one wild ride.

Better order a half dozen of those critters.

Five

The Galaxy on Grand Apartments
1:00 p.m.

The wiry man bustled through the maze of rooms in his apartment, nabbing stray newspapers and used dishes. Nester Arseneaux's efficiency amazed all that knew him, especially his parole officer. Almost a year passed since his release from the Texas prison he used to call home. The Galaxy on Grand Apartments never had a better manager. Lately though, the job irritated him.

Why? Take today, for example. Now, Nester made it a point never to judge anyone, but since Miss Shelby in 207 signed her lease a couple months ago, her shenanigans plain wore him out. Around six o'clock, his doorbell rings, and it's Miss Shelby—forgot her key again—what did she think he was, a camp counselor? He could barely see her face under that cowboy hat, and with all that makeup—what he could see looked good, very good, but still...

He hurried up the steps to her apartment and opened up the place. Things like this always happened on *Jeopardy* night. To his dismay and once again, the tinny doorbell chimed. "Yeah, yeah, Nester's on the way," he said.

He hustled to the door. Sweat trickled down his temples. *Why did he rush like this? No one ever left before he got there.* He twisted the knob and peered into the hall. "May I help you?"

"Arseneaux, when you going to clean the carpets? I thought it was supposed to be today."

Nester frowned and stared at the slender redhead. *Miss LaVerne, the busybody.* When she'd had a half bottle or so of bourbon in her, who didn't know her opinions on everything from bone china to the Vietnam War? "You came down here to ask me about rug day?"

"Yes and no."

"Well, which is it?"

"I wanted to know if today was the day for carpet cleaning, which apparently it wasn't, and I wanted you to ask Shelby Swain to keep that ruckus down in her living room."

Nester shrugged. "Ask her yourself. Y'all getting along fine?"

"She won't answer the door."

"Okay, okay. I'll call her. I need to see her about those rugs anyway. Couldn't believe the way it looked when I unlocked her apartment this afternoon. I do recall, her place is a fine mess."

"That must be the reason you sent those two Spanish looking guys to clean her rugs before you sent them over to my place. You know, Arseneaux, I was waiting for them."

"I don't know who or what you're talking about."

"Oh, I think you do. You just play favorites, that's all. And let me tell you something else. I am not the only one steamed about this. Other people saw them coming out of Shelby's apartment too. So, don't think you're going to get away with this."

He shook his head and ran his fingers through his wavy auburn hair. "Now, Miss LaVerne, I must excuse myself. *Jeopardy* is about to start, and I do need to tune in. Someday, real soon now, I'm gonna be on that show. I have to keep up with the questions—I mean the answers that are the questions."

"Sure, Arseneaux. You do that. So, am I getting my carpets cleaned tomorrow? Or do you have another favorite girl somewhere?"

"I'll have someone there bright and early. See you 'bout eight?"

"In the morning?"

"When else?"

"Shelby didn't have to get up at eight for rug day," Nester heard her mutter to herself, while she pattered down the hallway. *Good riddance.* Guess Miss LaVerne didn't like to start so early, but in his experience, no matter what the job, a person had to allow for the unexpected. Take the night he stole that car from the used car place, for example. How was he supposed to know it had such cheap tires? Some getaway car that was, couldn't take a little run-in with a lousy beer bottle, not to mention a security camera and an alarm that wouldn't shut up. Landed him in a Texas prison, doing five to eight. He sighed. Like he said, any job had hidden complications. Tomorrow would be no different.

Tonight, he focused on his true destiny: the *Jeopardy* Championship. Nester knew he was smart, maybe even smarter than anyone suspected or believed. If he won the *Jeopardy* championship, he would prove his worth, once and for all.

He crept closer to the television and studied the contestants' faces. None of them looked like a threat to him, not a chance. Question after question, he nailed the answer, in the form of a question, of course. He didn't mind answering questions, even when the answer was a question. Wait till they met him—Nester P. Arseneaux, First Place Champion.

Come to Papa.

He figured his application should come up for review any day now, complete with a personal reference from his parole officer. Still, some people acted so funny about a little hard time. Himself, he knew nobody was perfect—even someone like Shelby Swain in 207, or of course, Miss LaVerne. He could only hope the *Jeopardy* people felt the same way.

The Grapevine Detective Agency, 2:00 p.m.

"Suggs is a big boy, Mama. He doesn't need to call you every hour." Cobra puffed a cloud of smoke into the air, and leaned back in his chair.

For the first time since their introduction, Di ignored the smoke.

Cobra was her only confidante at the moment. "It's just not like him to not call."

"Well maybe he's just gonna drive down and back, real efficient like."

Di stared at him in confusion and disbelief.

"Okay, I didn't think so either." Cobra laughed. "Chances are, he ran into an old neighbor friend and they're chewing the fat about old times. You know how Elvin is. Or—you'll like this—maybe Vanna got sick."

"You think so?"

Cobra nodded. "See, I knew that suggestion would make you happy. You're as perky as a double shot expresso, or whatever it is you buy at that pricey joint that sells the foo–foo coffee you like so much."

"I don't think I sound happy. What makes you think I'm happy?"

"Maybe it's the big grin on your face."

"I am not grinning. I am just smiling. Can't I be happy?"

"Okay, you aren't grinning. You're just happy. Do you like that better? At any rate, there are a million ends to tie up when you sell property. You know that. Just look at all we had to do after the fire at the Jewel Arms."

Di nodded and stared into the distance. "Wasn't that something?"

"What? The Jewel Arms or what happened there?"

"Take your pick. For starters, I just couldn't believe what Cherie did to Elvin. How could she leave him for a vicious man like that awful Walter Hubble, and that obnoxious brother of his? I don't remember his name, but I remember the size of his belly."

"Arnold, Arno, something like that. Always eating some greasy potato chip and mayonnaise sandwiches or donuts. Man liked to die of a fat infection."

"You know, I don't think I ever knew anybody who ate that kind of food, not as much as he did." Di hesitated, then, finally spoke. "Don't even mention what they did to Tasha Weeks."

"They didn't get to Valerie, though, did they?"

At the mention of Cobra's girlfriend, Di's mood grew solemn. "No. No, they didn't."

"Shut you up, didn't I?"

"I just thought we were talking about Elvin, that's all."

"He'll call. Then, he'll say something you don't like, and you'll be mad that he called."

"How can you say something like that when it hasn't even happened yet?"

Cobra smirked and sucked a long drag from his cigarette. "Because it has happened. Time and again, Mama. Just waiting for another round." Cobra stubbed out his cigarette and frowned. "What are you doing?"

"I am calling Elvin. What's so unusual about that?" Di punched the buttons on her cell phone and pressed it to her ear. "Just a friendly little… Oh hi, El. Yeah, it's Di. How are you? What? Just wondering how things are going. You what?" Di frowned and crossed her legs. "What's her name?"

Cobra doubled over with laughter. "Just a friendly little call Di, remember?"

"Elvin, did you close on your house yet?"

Cobra watched while Di listened. He almost—almost felt sorry for her.

"Tomorrow? Why? Elvin, call me when you finish closing, will you? Will you do that? Bye." Di clicked the button and sighed. "I don't believe this. I do not believe this."

"What?"

"He picked up a hitchhiker."

"So? He picked me up, don't forget."

Di stared at Cobra for a moment, and considered his claim. "That's the truth, isn't it? But, he already knew you. That's not the same thing."

"Yes, but he didn't know he knew me until he talked to me and saw my tattoo. The thing about Suggs is, even if he hadn't known me, he would have picked me up and fed me so I wouldn't freeze to death.

Like it or not, that's Elvin. And, I don't know why you wouldn't like it." He smiled. "Unless, it's because this time, it's a woman. That's it, isn't it?"

"No. Well, maybe it is. I just don't trust it. It doesn't sound right."

"What do you mean?"

"I'll tell you what. When Elvin calls the next time, you talk to him. See what you think about this hitchhiker babe. Elvin says she's a tall blonde on her way to visit her mother."

"What else did she tell him?"

"Nothing."

Cobra laughed. "She got his number right off. I see what you mean. Well, she might be on her way to visit her mother. Question is, where is she coming from, and where's she headed after her visit?"

"That's what I'd like to know."

"Okay. Next time Suggs calls, put him on, and I'll talk to him." Cobra winked at the distraught redhead. "If his mama thinks she can hang on that long."

"I don't see that I have much choice in the matter."

"You catch on quick, Mama." Cobra pulled a cigarette from the crumpled pack. "Want a smoke?"

"Nope." She grinned at her rumpled companion. "Do me a favor?"

Cobra jammed the cigarette in his mouth, and reached for his lighter. "What now?"

"Put that back, and save your hot air."

"For what? If I run out of hot air, I am the one man in this state— hell, maybe the whole country—who has a ready supply of emergency hot air. Now, if you want to call Suggs again, just do it, so's I can smoke in peace."

"I don't want to call Elvin again."

"Oh yes, you do. You just don't want to admit it." Cobra stubbed out his cigarette. "Okay, I'll save my hot air for when Suggs calls. Are you happy?"

Di grinned. "Yeah."

Cobra shook his head. "Well, between you and Suggs, that means two out of three of us are happy—if we don't count Vanna."

"What if we do?"

"I guess that means I don't count."

"Guess that's what it means."

Cobra opened a fresh pack of cigarettes and put one in his mouth.

"What are you doing?"

"Seeing as how I don't matter, I'm going to use up my hot air, and—get this—be happy—at the same time." He lit the end of the cigarette and blew a puff of smoke into the air. "I can feel that hot air leaking right out of me as I speak." He grinned. "Guess you'll have to be the one with the hot air."

Di folded her arms across her chest and stared at the phone. "Guess I don't have a choice."

"You keep saying that."

Di stared at Cobra. "I do, don't I?"

Cobra leaned back in the chair and stubbed out his cigarette. "Better pack a bag, Mama. I got a feeling we're going to Memphis."

En route to Memphis, Tennessee

"Tell you what there, Shelby," Elvin said, "I got some licorice in the glove box if you're hungry. Vanna likes the cherry kind. I keep it there for emergencies."

Shelby frowned, and then giggled. "A candy emergency? Vanna has candy emergencies?"

"Shore 'nuf." *This girl really made him smile. Hadn't felt this good in a while, yeah.*

"You like to say that, don't you?"

"Say what?"

"Shore 'nuf. Your wife teach you to talk like that, did she? Elvin, did I say something wrong? You're married, is that it?"

Elvin stared at the road. "No ma'am. Not any more."

"What happened?"

"Ma'am, if you don't mind, I'd rather not say."

"Elvin?"

"Yes ma'am."

"Shore 'nuf."

He almost smiled—almost. The thought of Cherie was like a thundercloud. It would pass. It always did. "Well, here we are, Shelby, coming up on the dog track. Wisdom's south and east after we cross the river, or am I losing my handle?"

"Your what?"

"My handle. I've got a map in my head most of the time telling me where I am, where I'm going, how long I've got to get there and back. Cain't help it, ma'am. Holdover from 'Nam, I guess."

"You are one unusual guy, Elvin." Shelby smiled at him, and Elvin felt his stomach flip flop like a pancake turning on a hot griddle. *What was happening to him?*

"You probably won't believe this, but you're not the first woman to tell me that." Elvin squinted at the sign in the dusky shadows. "Are we coming up on Wisdom?" The blonde nodded. Elvin gawked at the mishmash of double–wide trailers and assortment of cars and pickups that occupied whatever spaces they could find. "And over there, that must be that El Dorado trailer place you're looking for. You sure this is it, Shelby?"

"Yeah, Elvin, it is. I wish I could tell you it wasn't, but…"

"You don't owe me nothing. Uh…"

"Shelby. Look Elvin, you're a nice guy, and I wish you the best. Just drop me off by the side of the highway, and I'll make my way up to the trailer court. Mama might be in, and then again, she might not be, I don't know." Shelby gestured to some stone steps that led to an overhead bridge. "Just pull over here. Right here will be fine."

"I don't feel right just dumping you out by the side of the road. Where I come from, a man takes a woman to the door and makes sure it shuts good and tight behind her."

"Elvin, I don't know what to expect, I told you. Some days my mama isn't herself."

"Ma'am, maybe I know a lot of strange people, but most days most of them aren't usually themselves. Believe me, whatever shape your mama's in, I can take it."

Shelby stared at him. "You are so different from any man I've ever known. Really."

"How's that?"

"You just seem so kind."

Elvin shrugged. "Why not?"

Shelby just shook her head. "Turn here, Elvin. Here's the exit. I must be dreaming."

Elvin stared straight ahead and gunned the engine. In his silence, he couldn't agree more.

The silver Caddy zoomed up the gravel drive, and turned onto El Dorado Lane. The brake lights glowed scarlet beneath the live oaks. Elvin Suggs couldn't recall why he had come to Memphis right now. Awake in a dream, he never wanted to wake up.

Six

The Grapevine Detective Agency
7:00 p.m.

"He should have called by now," Di said.

Cobra lit a fresh cigarette and blew a puff of smoke into the air. "Look, maybe he had trouble closing on the property, or maybe he changed his mind, or—"

Di jumped from the sofa as if it was on fire. "Changed his mind? Why would he do that? And anyway, Elvin promised he would call when he was done. You know something's up, Cobra. No, don't look at me like that. You know I'm right."

"You're acting like a crazy woman, you know that? Do you hear yourself?"

"El's in trouble. I can feel it."

"Feel it? Feel what?"

Di punched the numbers on the wall phone. "Memphis, Tennessee. Suggs, Elvin Suggs on Newell Street. Yes, I'll wait." Her hopeful expression faded. "Okay, thanks." She glanced at Cobra. "No answer at his house."

"What are you thinking? He wouldn't be there."

"Try his cell phone."

"I think you should wait until he calls us, but if you insist."

"Could you quit smoking for a few seconds, please?"

"That's two requests in as many minutes." Cobra stubbed out his cigarette. "But since you're not your usual charming self right now—"

"I am just fine."

Cobra rose from his chair and pressed the phone against his ear. "Yeah, is this the operator? Hey, how you doing? Great. Yeah, I need to get in touch with a guy named Suggs. That's Elvin Suggs, Memphis, Tennessee. I have his cell phone number, but do I dial the area code or what? Okay, bye." Cobra punched the numbers on the keypad and waited. "Hey Suggs, is that you?" Cobra listened for a few seconds. "You're kidding me. Hey, did you miss your closing? What do you mean you might not sell it? Have you lost your mind? Suggs, listen to me." Cobra turned to Di.

"I don't like the sound of this plan."

"He's in trouble, isn't he?" Di said.

"Well, if sitting in the El Dorado Trailer Court with a blonde angel and her blue eyes mean trouble, then Suggs has it."

Di and Cobra stared at each other.

"We shouldn't have let him go alone," Di said. "How long will it take to drive to Memphis?"

"Who's driving?"

"You are."

Cobra grinned. "I believe in the open road. You should know that up front."

Di loaded her Hi–Power pistol into her purse. "I'll do whatever it takes to bring Elvin back."

Cobra opened the front door. "After you." He gestured toward the curb, where Di's Suburban waited. He winked at Di. "We're going to get along just fine."

"*We* aren't what I'm worried about."

"Yeah? What's bothering you so danged much?"

"The last time Elvin referred to a blonde angel, he introduced me to Cherie."

"There was only one woman like that one."

"Until today, I thought so."

Cobra opened the door to the driver's side of the Suburban. "Now you got me worried. And when I'm worried, I drive kinda fast."

Di fastened her seatbelt. "I'm worried too. Kinda fast is exactly what I had in mind."

The Galaxy on Grand Apartments
Later that evening

Nester adjusted the volume on the television. He couldn't sleep. He never realized there were so many soap opera reruns in the middle of the night. He punched the buttons on the remote until he recognized one of them. There it was: *Hospital Daze.* The problem with that show was that Gloria and Gordon never said anything new. Ever.

Rad World wasn't much better, though Nester did enjoy the snappy dialogue and all of those flashy clothes. Nester couldn't remember that doctor's name, but he did recall the nifty way he smoked multiple cigarettes from designer ashtrays in strategic locations in his oversized, yet tastefully decorated office. He remembered the doctor's girlfriend's name, though. *Who could forget a name like Rominia Rumiñez?*

Lost in his thoughts, Nester barely heard the chime of the doorbell. He glanced at the clock on the kitchen wall. It was almost three a.m. "Who is it?"

The pounding grew louder. Nester opened the door, and faced a handsome man with an imposing presence. He looked familiar, but Nester was *sooo* tired. He couldn't quite place him. "Excuse me, sir," he said, "but, I'm sure I've seen you on television. Would you be the Reverend Jesse Jackson?"

Myles chuckled. "My name is Myles LaMour. I am an attorney. Tell me, does the Reverend Jackson visit you often?"

"Excuse me?"

"Forget it. My name is Myles LaMour. Please excuse the untimely intrusion—I don't usually do this sort of thing—but I've been unable to reach my ex-wife. You know, Miss Swain in #207? This is the manager's office, isn't it?"

"That would be me. Nester P. Arseneaux, Jr." He grasped Myles' hand and shook it. "People just call me Nester. So, you can't reach Miss Swain, huh? Well, it is three in the morning, Rev. She might be sleeping. You know, like I should be doing." Nester studied the man that stood before him. "To be fair here, I don't know you. I mean, I can't just let you into Miss Swain's apartment. Not without calling her first."

"Now, Nester, is it? I realize that you hardly know me. But, it seems that we have a mutual acquaintance."

"We do?"

"Does the name *Ronald Jupiter* sound familiar?"

Nester felt his stomach flip like a pancake in mid-air. He heard that Jupe got a life sentence somewhere in Texas. *And now this. Now this.*

"If it's the Ronald Jupiter I know, Counselor, he isn't much of a character reference. Might you be referring to a man named *Jupe*?" A tense moment lapsed. "For the record, he isn't my friend. I doubt he's one of yours."

"Is that a fact? Hmmm."

"How long have you known Jupe?"

"A couple of weeks, and I…"

"Come back after you've been in a space the size of a closet for a year with the guy. Then, we'll talk."

"Okay." Myles glanced over his shoulder. "Look, I'd like to know that Miss Swain is all right." He paused. "I have to believe that a man in your position would want to know the same thing."

Nester didn't reply. He couldn't believe the likes of this Myles LaMour, marching into his apartment building like this, telling him what he should and should not believe. No one told Nester Arseneaux what to believe. In fact, he wondered what LaMour already knew. In Nester's bleary-eyed estimation, LaMour knew far more than he was willing to admit.

Now that Nester thought about the whole thing, the last tenant in Miss Swain's apartment was a murder victim—not that Nester told her as much. Besides, nobody ever proved anything, or solved the case for that matter. All the same, Nester thought he would keep that intriguing tidbit to himself.

"Yeah, okay. I'll take you upstairs. But, don't think it's because of Jupe. And, I'll give you a little advice, Rev. I wouldn't refer to Jupe as a friend." Nester paused. He seemed to be deep in thought. "You know, Counselor, I just have to ask you something. When you go out on a case in the middle of the night, do you always dress up like that?"

Myles looked genuinely puzzled. "Yes, I do."

Nester nodded. "I thought so." He grabbed his master key ring. "Okay, LaMour. Let's go on up."

Seven

The Galaxy on Grand Apartments
#206

LaVerne Piece inspected her nail polish and slurped a Diet Coke. Nowadays, she lived on the settlement she received from her botched liposuction. Her "tummy tuck" never tucked, but she had to admit, her thighs did look a lot trimmer; and, she met some fantastic men along the way. There was the surgeon, of course—before the lawsuit—and her lawyer, Myles LaMour, and a few of his partners…

Wait a minute. Footsteps pounded on the stairs outside her door. Motionless, she sat on the worn sofa and listened to the jangle of keys, and the jumble of hushed voices, whispering muffled words in the darkness.

She tightened the sash of her terrycloth robe and crept to the door, pressing her ear against the thin wood. *Did she dare open it, just a bit? No, too risky.* Somewhere, a door creaked. She was sure she recognized the voices. One belonged to Nester Arseneaux, and the other, well, she would swear it belonged to her fine–looking attorney, Myles LaMour. Drawers slammed and closets opened and closed. *Why were they poking around Shelby's apartment?* LaVerne sipped more Diet Coke to fortify herself. Actually, she hadn't seen Myles LaMour in, oh, maybe a year. She'd get dressed right now.

Now, where were those black pants? She inspected the stack of clothes piled on an armchair in the corner, peeling each piece like the layers of an onion. A roach scampered under a pair of jeans, and she recoiled in disgust. How many times had she implored Arseneaux to call an exterminator? *Worthless, that's what he was.* She grabbed the jeans between her thumb and forefinger and shook them. Actually, they seemed alright, but as LaVerne knew, things could turn on a dime. The proverbial New York minute knew her well.

She stepped into the hall and tapped on the door of #207.

Apartment #207

The two men heard the tapping on the door.

"Ignore it, Arseneaux," Myles said. "This is no time for company." He gawked at the corpse splayed on the stained carpet. "Nope, that is not my Shelby. No way."

Nester scratched his head. A few seconds lapsed while he considered a question for his answer. "Well then, Rev, who might she be?"

The tapping on the door grew more insistent.

"What do I do, Rev?"

"LaMour. My name is Myles LaMour, Attorney at Law." He reached into his back pocket and retrieved his wallet. He slipped a cardboard square into Nester's bony fingers. "Here's my business card."

Nester squinted at the card. "Impressive artwork. I especially like the skull and bones there at the top, right next to your face. The scales of justice are a nice touch, too. Quite becoming, really—and so flattering to the complexion. So tell me, how is it that you came to know Miss Swain?"

"I am her...well, I was, her ex–husband." He shook his head. "Seeing this...I just don't know what to think."

"No kidding."

"No kidding." Myles took a deep breath, and opened the door, ever so slightly. "LaVerne, what a nice surprise!"

"Myles! You look great. Is..." She stood on her tiptoes, and struggled to get just a peek at the interior of the apartment. "Is everything alright? I heard so much noise, I thought I should come over, and…AAAAGH!"

Myles grabbed her by the shoulders and pulled her inside the apartment. Nester slammed the door.

"You'll upset the other tenants, Miss LaVerne," Nester said. "Hush yourself."

"You've got to stop screaming," Myles said. "It's not helping anyone. Especially Shelby."

"But Myles, Shelby's deee…" All at once, LaVerne stopped crying and stared at the corpse's bloated face. "That's not Shelby."

"I don't think so, either," Myles said.

"For one thing, Shelby had triple pierced ears. And, she just got a rose tattoo on the back of her…"

"Please keep those things to yourself, LaVerne," Myles said, "I will need you to make a statement." He turned to Nester. "We need to get this lady identified and moved to a better place than the floor of a strange apartment. It's not decent, nor is it good for reputation of this building, which is already…"

"Already what?" Nester said.

Myles decided to forego any further comments regarding the lurid reputation of the Galaxy on Grand Apartments. Events spoke for themselves, after all, and what they didn't say, the newspapers usually did. "I happen to know a very sharp homicide detective. If it's all right with you, I think it's time I give him a call, and have him come over here. His name is Reggie Combs, and we've worked together before on a few cases. I'm sure you'll like him."

"Sure. Sure thing, LaMour." Nester stared at him for a few moments. "Whatever you think is best. If you're absolutely sure this isn't Miss Swain." He moved a bit closer. "Are you sure?"

Myles ignored the question. At this moment, his cell phone appeared to be attached to his ear. "I'd like to speak to Reggie Combs, please. Sergeant Reggie Combs." His gaze wandered to the corpse on the rug, then to Nester's face. "Last chance, Arseneaux. Any idea who the lady is?"

"LaMour, I told you. I thought it was Miss Shelby, but now—now, I'm not so sure," Nester whispered.

"I was wondering about that," LaVerne said.

"Why is that? I said I'm not sure."

"Why did you open the door to her apartment if you weren't sure who she was? You let her in, didn't you?"

"I don't know what you're talking about, Miss LaVerne."

"Arseneaux, didn't you tell me that Shelby Swain stopped by your office last night because she locked herself out? You said that. I know you did. You also said the place was a mess, and..."

"Well, yes, but..." Nester's face looked flushed, even in the shadows.

"What do you mean *but?* Did you know that woman, Arseneaux?"

Nester continued to whisper. "I thought it was Miss Shelby, with that hat and her long blonde hair. But now that I look closer, I'm not quite sure. I only met Miss Shelby the one time, when she signed the rental papers. I—"

Myles faced Nester and LaVerne. "Please, save your remarks for Sergeant Combs. He'll be here soon enough. He's on the line now." His back stiffened when he spoke. "Reggie! It's Myles, Myles LaMour. Good to hear your voice, man. Yeah. Things are good. Well, actually... no, they're not so good. I'm over here at the Galaxy Apartments. Yeah, the Galaxy on Grand. You know the place. I'm here with Mr. Arseneaux, the Manager. You want to speak with him? Sure, when you get here. Miss Gains? No, I haven't seen her tonight. Should I? Didn't think you wanted that kind of trouble tonight. Nope. Neither do I." Myles paced around the small kitchen. The crimson spatters on the sunny yellow paint stopped him cold. "Well, tonight there's a different blonde in trouble. Yeah. That's why I called. Well, Reg, this blonde is dead. From the looks of things, she's been that way for a while."

Nester glanced at Mrs. Piece. "Hear that, Miss LaVerne? If I were you, I'd keep your red hair."

Myles turned to face Nester again. "Please, Mr. Arseneaux. Such comments are inappropriate, especially under the circumstances." Again, he pressed the cell phone to his ear. "Sure Reg, I'll wait till you get here. Bye."

"Mr. LaMour," Nester said, "I was only saying that Miss LaVerne might be safer with her red hair. You say this blonde isn't Miss Shelby. Okay. Do you know who she is?"

"Me? No, I absolutely do not. But, a client of mine might have mentioned her. I am not at liberty to discuss the matter, Mr. Arseneaux."

Nester smirked at his nebulous reply. "I figured as much. Well then, we all can just wait till your Sergeant arrives. And then what do we do?"

"I'm sure that Sergeant Combs will have some concrete ideas along those lines, Mr. Arseneaux."

"I was just wondering something," LaVerne said. "If that's not Shelby, then where is she? Shouldn't she be getting off work about now?"

"That's why I came here in the first place," Myles said. "She didn't answer her phone."

Nester, Myles and LaVerne stared at the blonde on the floor.

Nester felt like a killer.

Eight

The El Dorado Trailer Court, that same evening

Gilda Shultz loved to shoot her revolver, but the cleanup was such a nuisance. The cleaning solvent and gun oil somehow offended her coupon–clipping, card playing pals, and so she usually did it alone. She loved to talk, but with no one to listen, it could be such a solitary activity.

One glance at her targets from the day's practice, and her soul gushed with pride. How she wished she could flaunt her victory! One bullseye after another! Pretty darned good for a seventy–five year old widow, if she did say so herself.

Now, she sat at the kitchen table covered with yesterday's newspaper, and wiped down the parts of the old Colt with the corner of a rag. She inhaled deeply and grinned. *Nothing like the smell of that cleaner.* Personally, she liked Hoppe No. 9, but some people—

The drone of unfamiliar voices buzzed in Gilda's ears. She peered into the shadows and spotted a tall, muscular man, nice–looking by the way, accompanied by a slender blonde. At first, they seemed to be headed in the direction of her trailer; instead, they rapped on Letha Swain's door. *Some people got all the luck. Go figure.* Gilda wished with all her heart that someone would visit her sometime.

Now, she heard the jangle of keys, accompanied by more voices. "Mama! Hey! Open up in there! It's Puddin'!"

Mama? Who was Puddin'? Was Letha someone's mama? In all their conversations, Letha never mentioned a daughter or a son. To

Gilda, it sure looked like she had one of each. *Some people got all the luck. Well, if Letha wasn't home, maybe they'd like to come over and visit her, how about that?*

She hobbled to the front door and cracked it, ever so slightly. "Miss? Mister? Don't think Letha's home." She gawked at the two visitors. *The blonde was stunning, oh my. And the man, well, he was a hunk; it had been a while since she'd seen that kind of man.* "Y'all hungry?"

The blonde looked startled. Gilda didn't understand that part— until she realized she was staring at the gun in her wrinkled hand. "Oh my, I forgot to put away my thumbbuster."

She began to shut the door when the man said, "That's a nice gun you have there, ma'am." It was the voice of a Memphis native, Gilda felt certain. She opened the door, and addressed the man with the pleasant expression on his face.

"Why, thank you. It belonged to my daddy."

"That critter's got some history, don't it? From here, it looks like a 4 ¾ inch Colt Single Action Army."

A wide smile spread across Gilda's face. "That it is."

"You wouldn't be looking to sell it now, would you?"

"Oh, nossir."

"Well, when I heard it belonged to your daddy, I reckoned that would be the case. I respect that, really do. Tell me something, though. If you ever decide you want to sell it, why, I'd sure appreciate your consideration."

"Why, that's right decent of you, sir." Gilda tried to focus on his features, size him up, but the shadows made it next to impossible for her feeble eyes to discriminate much of anything. "You're a collector, are you?"

"No ma'am. I'm a, well…these days, I own a detective agency back in St. Louis. I won't say it's home, because Memphis will always be my home. But, I have to say, St. Louis has been mighty good to me."

"A detective agency. My, oh my. That just sounds so exciting," Gilda said.

"It can be that," Elvin said. "What's wrong, Shelby?"

All of a sudden, Gilda noticed the blonde seemed anxious to leave. "Something wrong?" she said.

"No," she said. "It's just that Mama isn't home, and I don't want to keep Mr. Suggs here any longer than I already have. Elvin, what do I owe you for the gas?"

"Shelby, what's wrong?" Elvin said. "You look a little sick, girl. You all right? You know, it was probably those Barn Busters we ate. Vanna and me feel just fine, though. Don't we, Vanna?"

Gilda craned her neck so that she could see the interior of Elvin's car. "You have another girl with you? All I see is a whopper of a dog."

"Oh, you mean Vanna," Elvin said. "I guess we should let you meet her too. She shouldn't have to wait by herself in the car all the time."

"Well, I would hope not," Gilda said. "You know, some things a girl never forgets. I used to hate it when my late husband made me wait in the car."

"Hear that, Shelby?" Elvin said.

"Yeah, Elvin. I heard."

"You sure you don't want to me to call you tomorrow morning?" Elvin said. "You never know. Just getting into town and all, you might need something. You sure you're okay by yourself?"

"Yes, I'm sure. I've caused you enough trouble for one night. Before you go, you should let me pay you for gas."

"No ma'am, that's just not my way. I'll tell you how we'll handle this. When you find somebody who needs a kindness, why then, you just think of me and pass it on. Tell them Elvin Suggs sent you. Good luck to you now." Elvin descended the rickety wooden steps and turned to face her. "Miss Shelby, I wish tonight didn't have to end."

Gilda noticed the fear in the blonde's eyes. Something was bothering that gal, she decided. Something she couldn't forget. *Hmmm.* Gilda decided she wouldn't put her pistol away just yet.

Nine

Nester Arseneaux's apartment

Reggie scanned the comments he recorded in his black notebook. He believed Arseneaux's statement pertinent to the blonde's murder. Yet, the remarks from everyone else in the room raised his suspicions. For one thing, Reggie believed in eye contact. Arseneaux was the only one who seemed comfortable with that interview technique. Reggie didn't yet understand the reason for Myles and Laverne's trepidation, but before this case was over, he would. He promised himself that he would.

Everything about Myles's demeanor puzzled him, particularly the Nevada driver's license that he found in the pocket of the victim's jeans. The license identified a victim by the name of Claire Ireland, though it didn't appear that she drove herself to the Galaxy Apartments. Nester said the parking lot had been empty most of the evening, since it was Saturday night and all. Reggie remarked on her uncanny resemblance to Shelby Swain; indeed, they could have been twin sisters.

For some reason, Reggie felt certain that Attorney LaMour knew far more about Claire Ireland and Shelby Swain, individually and together, than he wanted to admit. He also sensed Myles's reluctance to discuss his stash of information, so unlike the Myles LaMour he thought he knew so well. But, he reminded himself, given enough time, everyone and everything changes. He supposed that even he, Reggie, had changed over the past few years.

Certainly, LaVerne Piece warranted further questioning. Reggie had a hunch that a woman who looked and walked like LaVerne knew something about everything and everybody she met—and Reggie's hunches were the stuff of the famous office wagers. Reggie climbed the steps to #206, and rapped on the orange door. Even in the shadows, it glowed like the dying embers of a blazing flame. With luck on his shoulder, he decided to ask her a few questions.

LaVerne Piece's apartment

For the past two years, LaVerne lived at the Galaxy Apartments, ever since her late husband Elwood, rest his smokin' soul, died in a house fire. He loved to smoke in bed, especially when LaVerne went to the gambling boats on Thursday nights.

One Thursday night, LaVerne didn't come home. Elwood got upset and chain–smoked two cigarettes at a time, until one dropped into the tangled sheets. The whole mess smoked Elwood and the house to death. The next morning, LaVerne didn't have Elwood or a house. Myles LaMour, her attorney at the time, located Apartment #206 faster than a speeding…well, after the whopper legal settlement and the quicky apartment setup, Myles was Superman, at least in LaVerne's book.

The Galaxy on Grand wasn't the classiest complex in the city, but a lady like her ought to be able to find a safe place to live without paying an arm or a leg…or a body. Which is what LaVerne told that homicide detective, oh, about an hour ago now. And, she thought that quite possibly, he believed her. She wasn't entirely shocked by his presence on her doorstep. She figured he'd have some stuff to settle privately—*didn't they all? Might as well get this over with.*

"Sergeant! Having a problem?" LaVerne tilted her head ever so slightly and flashed her best smile.

"Don't know yet, Mrs…" Reggie flipped through the notebook pages.

"Piece. LaVerne Piece. That's P–i–e–c–e."

Reggie scribbled the note in his book. "May I come in? This will only take a few minutes."

"Well, it's so late, and I told you everything I know, Sergeant Combs."

"I just have a few questions. I'd like to go home, Miss Piece."

"Mrs."

"Ma'am?"

"It's Mrs. Piece."

"Pardon me. Mrs. Piece. I'll repeat my request. May I come in?"

LaVerne sighed. "Sure. Fine. I don't have anything new to say, I swear. But, you seem to think I do. So, come on in. I wasn't exactly expecting company, so you'll have to excuse the cockroaches."

She gestured to a loveseat, covered in piles of newspapers. "Have a seat."

Reggie frowned at the stacks of paper. "I'll stand for now, thanks. Tell me, Mrs. Piece, what is your relationship to Myles LaMour?"

LaVerne nodded in a sly manner and chuckled. "So, that's it. You think Myles and I have something going on?"

"Do you?"

"What does it matter if we do or we don't?"

"Please answer the question, Mrs. Piece."

"Why don't you ask Myles? I thought you two were old buddies and all that."

"Mrs. Piece, do we need to go downtown to my office?"

"Look, I'll tell you how it is. And then, you decide what we need to do. Because my life is not so black and white, okay? I met Myles when I was married to Elwood Cash, about, um, three years ago. Well, I got a little porky, and Elwood suggested I get liposuction, which I did, but the doctor showed up drunk to the operation. The surgery was a disaster."

"You seem to be doing well now."

"Well, of course. I asked around and found a better doctor after that. But, at the time, I needed a good personal injury attorney. Myles is a very charming man, as you may have noticed. Or not. Anyway, he was married to Shelby at the time. But, nevertheless, we went out for a few drinks and whatever..."

"Whatever?"

"We'd go to the gambling boat on Thursday night. Elwood loved to watch that show ER and smoke in bed, and one night, well, he burned himself up, along with our house. Myles helped me through it. He even helped me rent this place."

"Really? So, you like it here?"

"Arseneaux is a little shady, but he's usually around when you need him."

"Shady? Exactly what do you mean?"

"Well, you know...he's done some time, and he's on parole. I was surprised that Myles didn't know that. Or at least he didn't mention it when he hired him. "

"Whoa. Wait just a minute. Myles hired Arseneaux?"

"Oops." LaVerne covered her mouth with her hand. "That's really confidential. Arseneaux doesn't know that Myles owns this building."

"I see. Well, actually, no, I don't. Not at all. Tell me, do you still see Mr. LaMour?"

"Yeah, sure, from time to time. You don't just drop someone after five years of good times. I don't, anyway. What exactly are you after here?"

"I'm after a killer, for starters. That's what I do."

"You don't really think Myles would kill anyone." LaVerne paused. "Do you?"

"Goodnight, Mrs. Piece. I'll be in touch." Reggie strode through the orange door and into the damp night air. He didn't know what he believed, but after tonight, he absolutely knew one thing. There was much more to learn about Myles LaMour and LaVerne Piece than he ever imagined.

Myles shrugged and hustled up the stairs to the second floor. He glimpsed a shadow lingering in the hall, and turned the corner. LaVerne waited for him in the darkness.

She didn't speak until Myles shut the flimsy door to her apartment. She took a deep breath and her head pounded. "I didn't do anything, I swear, Myles. You believe me, don't you?"

Myles gazed at the ceiling. "Sure. Sure, I do."

His attitude wouldn't convince a detective, a jury or a goldfish of her innocence. Of that, LaVerne felt certain. And there was something else on her mind.

Did Myles know about her fresh baked split from Jupe? If he ever doubted Jupe's alibis, LaVerne understood. Herself, she never believed any of them, except the most incredible ones. Those were consistently, and without exception, the truth.

It would be only a matter of time before Myles discovered the minefield of her romantic past. *Who did she think she was kidding?*

Ten

The Lounge by Maurice
St.Louis, Missouri

Eduardo steered the rental car onto the gravel parking lot and slammed on the brakes. He stared at the aged brick structure in disbelief. "Thees muss be the place."

Santy shook his head. "You make a wrong turn, Eduardo. Where you get your informacíon, eh? Who tell you come to thees place?"

Eduardo stared straight ahead when he spoke. "Who you think? Arseneaux."

"Then Arseneaux, he lie to us, eh? Thees is not the Galaxy Aparmenns."

"We are not going to stay here, Santy."

"No?"

"No. Of course not. I went to the Galaxy on Grand Apartments and I found this Nester Arseneaux. He say he don't know any Kimmy Cruz. I ask him, does he know where I could fine someone who know how to find the Kimmy. I tell him I hear from Jupiter Ron that she call herself *Krystal Light*.

"Arseneaux, he hear that, and he tell me to come to this address and ask for Mr. Moe Reeze. He say Mr. Reeze know all about Kimmy here, Kimmy there, Krystal this and Krystal that. He say he can help us. Ha! We are in the right place. It must be true. The GPS, she says so." He looked closer at the weeds that surrounded the entrance to the Lounge by Maurice. "This place, you are *muy correcto*. It's not right.

Sometimes Santy, there is no explanacíon for the truth."

"I just theenk Kimmy would not sing here or dance here, or—"

"Why not? She work at El Gallo Loco, din't she? Look Santy, juss let me talk, hokay? I know why we are here and that is enough."

"You're the boss. What you think Arturo would say?"

"He told me get Kimmy Cruz and bring her back to him—alive. She should pay for her sins."

"What she do exacly?"

"She kill Arturo's brother Hector. She take his gun. Then, she steal *mucho, mucho dinero* from Arturo's safe."

"Oh boys." Santy covered his eyes with his thick fingers. "Oh boys."

"What if we have to kill her?"

"We don't have to kill her."

"Why not?"

"Arturo say, it is his place to finish his business."

Eduardo laughed but his eyes looked as cold as marbles. He opened the car door and stepped into the drive. A cloud of dust swirled around him. "C'mon, Santy. It is late. We will talk to Mr. Reeze."

The Lounge by Maurice, same time

From the beginning, Maurice didn't like the looks of that shiny gold car. Where cars, people, and his fine business were concerned, he knew who and what belonged in the neighborhood—and who and what did not. In his book, such was the law of survival. So, when the golden Mercury squealed into the gravel lot next to his lounge, Maurice appeared, beer bottle in hand, looking like an irritated lion with a thorn in its paw. For a second, he paused and stared at the faces of the men, now standing beside the Mercury.

"What do y'all want?" he said, and took a swig from the bottle. "We're getting ready to open up for the night." He noticed how the men looked at each other, almost quizzically, almost as if they couldn't understand him. From this distance, he could barely discern the outline of their faces—some brand of Mexicans, he thought. But, Maurice didn't know Spanish; why would he? He didn't even know anybody that spoke any Spanish. *Didn't he have enough problems keeping the help in line?* He still hadn't found a girl to replace Shelby, and that—now, that—cost him big money, by the hour. For some reason, he felt nervous about getting any closer to that car.

Eduardo ascended the wide steps with confidence.

"Ah, Meester Reeze. I am referred by Mr. Arseneaux." Eduardo grinned like a cat that just cornered a mouse. "You know thees girl, eh?" He flashed a recent photo of Kimmy, and just as quickly, replaced it in his bulging wallet.

"Man, I can't see that itty bitty thing." Maurice eyed him with caution.

"Time is of the essence, Mr. Reeze."

"If I know one thing, it's this: Nester don't hurry for nobody. So, don't get funny on me. My name ain't Moe or Reeze. The name is Maurice White. You sure Arseneaux sent you?"

Eduardo nodded. "Arseneaux, *sí*. The Galaxy on Grand Apparmens. *Mi nombre es Eduardo.* And theese is Santy."

Maurice stared at the strangers. *Hard to believe Arseneaux would have anything to do with these two greaseballs.* "Lissen up. How y'all know Nester?"

Santy's fingers brushed his coat aside to reveal the butt of a pearl handled Colt .38 Super tucked inside the waistband of his trousers. The bright nickel–plated metal glinted in the neon light. Maurice gawked at the pistol, and then, at the Mercury, now parked a few feet from them.

Eduardo spoke first. "Arseneaux, we meet a friend of his in Texas, in the halfway house." He flashed his best barracuda smile. "Saint Francis. Now, *por favor*..."

"Look, Tex, let me see that picture." Maurice nodded. "So, you two know Krystal, do you?"

Eduardo's face lit up like a Christmas tree. "*Sí!* Krystal Light? Kimmy? You know her, eh?"

"I don't know nothing about any Kimmy. Get that part straight. Krystal worked here a little while, maybe two months. Not long. Nice legs, if you ask me." He tipped his head and drained the last of the beer from the bottle. "Always talking to her ex about something. And then, some guy name Jupe showed up, and she be gone with the wind."

At the mention of Jupe's name, Santy's hand patted the gun.

"Hey, take it easy. I take it you guys know this Jupe character, too." Maurice grinned. "Well, I ain't got nothing to hide. What do you want to know?"

"We want to fine Krystal Light," Eduardo said. "We miss her."

"Yeah, well, that's between you and her."

"Where she go?"

Maurice chewed on his lip. "Don't exactly know." He sensed the tension between them. "Tell you what. For a few bucks, I could possibly remember a few things. Possibly."

"You remember the lass time you see her?" Santy said.

"We need to know, Meester Reeze," Eduardo said.

"I tole you before. It's Maurice. And I haven't seen Shelby for a coupla days now."

"Who is Shelby?" Eduardo looked confused.

"Krystal." Maurice frowned. "You know, Shelby."

"Make up your mine," Santy said. "Which she gonna be?"

"Didn't you know her real name?" Maurice said. "Don't tell me you thought it was Krystal Light." He leaned back and laughed out loud. "That's a good one."

"Mr. Reeze, we are not unnerstanning you." Eduardo reached in the pocket of his overcoat and retrieved a wad of bills. Maurice stared at the stack of bills as if he had never seen cash up close and personal. "Can you tell us where to fine Miss Krystal Light? Or no?" He peeled the bills as if they were layers of an onion. "You know Santy, it is soch a shame, when one can pay, but the informacíon, she is not there."

"Okay, Lissen up," Maurice said. He gestured with the beer bottle in his hand. "Y'all are telling me that all you want to know is where Krystal went, like her address? And you want to pay me for that?" His eyes narrowed. "Why you want to see her so bad?"

"We like her," Eduardo said.

"*Sí*," Santy said. "We want to take her to deener."

"So, Mr. Reeze," Eduardo said, "what you think, eh?"

"Hmmm." Maurice thought they were liars, dressed in sheep's clothing. But the dishwasher in the kitchen was broke and so was he; five, maybe six of those C-notes in the taller one's hands, would erase his problem, along with these *cucarachas*. After all, all they wanted was her address…

"Okay, I got her forwarding address back in the office," Maurice said. "I owe her a paycheck, matter of fact." *Besides that, what was he worrying about?* They would probably never meet up with Krystal or Shelby. "So, what's this address worth to y'all?"

Eduardo pursed his thin lips. "Five hunred?"

Maurice ogled the thick stack of bills. He knew Mex here could pay more. But, he asked himself, would he? Well, he would never know if he didn't ask for more. Besides that, he didn't like these guys. He needed more dough to assuage his conscience. Through a small window by the bar, he caught a glimpse of the gold Mercury. Beneath the glow of the streetlight, it gleamed and glimmered like a diamond in a cave.

"Seven hundred," Maurice said. "That's my final offer."

Santy grumbled something about Arturo and thieves. Eduardo did not look happy. Still, the tall one peeled seven C-notes from the stack and offered them to Maurice. "You are very 'spensive, Mr. Reeze."

"Yes," Maurice said. "But, I'm the real thing. Just like gold. Fourteen karat and some change."

Eduardo remained businesslike. "Now, you will give us the address, Mr. Reeze. We are on a tight schedule, eh Santy?"

Santy patted the gun. "*Sí.*"

Maurice mounted the steps to the front door, the C–notes firmly in his grasp. "I'll be right back, y'all."

"Don't worry, Meester Reeze. We are right behind you." Eduardo grinned.

Somehow, Maurice already knew that part.

Memphis, Tennessee, 12:30 a.m.

"You know, Red, we would have been here a lot faster—and, I mean like lightning, baby—if you hadn't made me stop twice already." Cobra opened the window of the Suburban and blew a puff of smoke into the twilight air. "But, here we are, rolling into Memphis in the dark."

"It is not that dark, and Elvin Suggs, wherever he is, won't be hard to find. Wherever he goes, we always hear him. Remember the day Don died?" As soon as the words escaped her mouth, Di wished they hadn't. Back in '68, Elvin had been the one to find her late husband Don, in the jungle in 'Nam; Elvin witnessed his last words and delivered Don's Browning Hi–Power pistol to Di—his final gift to her. One glance at Cobra scared her. Memories like these always provoked one of his anxiety attacks. Never failed. The expression on his face confirmed her worst fear. "I'm sorry, Cobra. I shouldn't have said that. Are you alright?"

"Where are we now?" Cobra's skin turned a ghostly shade of pale. "Di, I need a pack of smokes."

"You're asking me to buy them for you?"

"Well, I looked around, and it appears that you're my only choice, Red."

"You need something to eat." She pulled off the highway. "Let's grab some dinner first."

"C'mon, I'm broke. A pack of smokes is my dinner."

"It's not going to be mine. Look over there. You like catfish?"

"Never had it. But anyplace that's called Memphis Chop Suey Catfish can't make up its mind what it's serving. Where are we again?"

"We're just over the state line in Tennessee, home of Graceland and Elvin. Anything is possible tonight."

"What about that barbecue place over there? Suggs always used to talk about taking Cherie out for barbecue."

"Yeah, what's your point?"

"Well, they must have liked something about it."

"They usually fought over barbecue sandwiches, if you ask me."

Cobra grinned. "Sounds like it'd be the perfect place for us then, don't it?"

Eleven

Nester Arseneaux's apartment

"Good to see you there, Jupe," Nester said. "Have a pizza with me? I'm getting ready to watch *Jeopardy*. Remember how we used to watch *Jeopardy* at St. Francis? We always got the answers, remember? I mean, the questions that were the answers."

"I remember everything about that place. I wish I could forget about St. Francis and everything I did before that. But, you know what I really wish? I wish everyone else would forget about all of that, too. Everywhere I go, people say, oh, you did some hard time? Well, no job for ex-cons, sorry. What am I supposed to do with a whole lot of sorry? I can't eat sorry, Nester."

"I know, I know. I've got almost a year in myself, Jupe, but, you watch, I'm gonna clean up on *Jeopardy*. I'm gonna be so rich up to here, people gonna be sorry they treated Nester Arseneaux like a loser. Hey, what they don't know is, these days, it takes brains to be a successful criminal."

"You know something, Arseneaux? You're right. By the way, how'd you land this job?"

"Dumb luck." Nester chomped on the crispy crust of the pizza, and began to chew the cheesy goo with his mouth open. "What's eating you, Jupe? Somethin' is. Hey, you need something to eat?"

"I need a place to stay, Nester. I don't have any place to go." Jupe paused and took a deep breath. "Think I could stay here for awhile?"

Nester swallowed a mouthful of pizza and thought for a moment.

"Listen to me, Jupe. Do you have a job? Because I can't accept an application for an apartment if you don't write something down where it says 'employment.' Say, where are you living now?"

"Last night I slept in the bathroom at the library. Sometimes, I stay in the park. But, I can't keep this up forever, taking baths out of a sink in a gas station restroom. And, you're wrong about the job part." He examined the black grime beneath his ragged fingernails. "I have lots of jobs, Nester. Just not the nine to five variety."

Nester stared at Jupe. "What do you mean?"

"If the work pays, I do it. It's really pretty simple."

"How do I explain that? The kind of people that read the apartment applications, Jupe, they want to see some kind of job that they recognize. Like, for example, maybe you could say you work in a dry cleaning store, or a bowling alley. Maybe you could say you deliver pizza. Or you could even say you wash people's hair in a beauty shop. Jobs like these kind of jobs, they can relate to you. See what I mean?"

"Nester, I never had any of those kinds of jobs. Can you see me working in a beauty shop? I don't even like pizza. And, I don't know the first thing about bowling or dry cleaning. Can't you figure something out? You are the management here. Who's gonna bother you about stuff like that, anyway?"

Nester shuffled over to the television set and adjusted the volume. "I never know what's going to happen here. Besides, the only place open right now is Miss Shelby's place and…"

"I'll take it. You can't rent it anyway."

"It's got bloodstains all over the living room carpet."

"So, I stay outta the living room. I don't think it's a big deal if you don't. C'mon Nester, I need a place to hang out, just till I can get my stuff together. Besides, who's gonna know?"

Nester stared at him for a minute. "Here's the problem."

"What problem?"

"The place is right next to Miss LaVerne's apartment."

"Who?"

"Miss LaVerne is the nosiest woman on the planet. Maybe in the entire universe. She will bug you to death."

"If it's the same LaVerne Piece that I know, I can handle her questions."

Nester rose from the lounge chair and hustled into the kitchen. He cracked the door to the fridge and stared at the meager contents. "Want a Dr. Pepper?"

"Arseneaux, I promise you, if you let me stay up in #207, you won't be sorry. I might even be some help to you."

"I'm gonna tell you something. Are you listening? Yesterday, a couple of rough looking Spanish type guys came by here, looking for a woman named Kimmy Cruz. Now, why would they think I know anyone like that? I'll tell you what, as long as I've been here, I haven't rented an apartment to anybody with a name like Kimmy Cruz. Not that I wouldn't. I just haven't had the occasion. Couldn't convince them of that, though. To tell you the truth, they made me very nervous."

"Yeah," Jupe said. "I'll bet." *They make me nervous, too.*

"The thing is, Jupe, since I moved in here, there's been two murders, both in #207. I don't think they're related, but still, watch your step up there. I'm not kidding."

"Who'd want to kill me?"

"You mess up my parole, I'll kill you myself. You understand?"

"Yeah, Nester, but..."

"No *buts* about it. I'm almost outta here. I am on my way to the *Jeopardy* championship and a whole new life, where the present and future are what count, and the past stays in the past. And Jupe, let me tell you, it better stay that way."

"You're serious."

"Like a rubber crutch."

"Okay."

The theme music to *Jeopardy* blared from the television. "*Jeopardy* time," Nester said. "Look Jupe, you can stay up in 207 if you want. Just don't bother me during *Jeopardy*. And don't mess anything up in there.

The key is on the hook by the door."

"Thanks, Nester. You won't be sorry. I promise." Jupe snatched the key to #207 and tiptoed out of the apartment. The aromas of stale French fries and cigarette smoke filled the narrow entrance hall. Never mind, he thought, making his way to the second floor. It still smelled better than a gas station restroom, though a few of them were so clean, they surprised him.

Quiet. It was so quiet in here, he thought. Jupe hadn't had this much time to think in a quiet place for a year, maybe four or five. Was this the way that other people lived? *Naw.*

He jammed the key into the lock of #207, and twisted the knob. The door opened without resistance. *Strange, very strange. Arseneaux must have forgotten to lock it after the cops left.*

The furniture looked expensive. White leather sofa, glass coffee table, carved lamps. *Somebody had money.* He sat down on the sofa. It felt unnatural to sit on something white, especially leather.

The phone rang. *Where was it?* Jupe heard it, but he couldn't see it. He looked at the kitchen wall. *Nope.* The long hall led to a bedroom, he supposed. *Ringing. Ringing.* He wasn't used to the shrill sound and it pierced his ears. He almost decided not to pick up the receiver when he realized the identity of the caller. *It's Arseneaux calling to see if I got in. Yeah, okay. I'll pick it up.*

He put the receiver to his ear. The laughter rippled across the wire.

"Who is this?" Jupe looked around the bedroom as if the shadows might supply the answer. Alone in the darkness, Jupe shivered under a blanket of silence.

The laughter continued.

"Who the hell is this?"

"Kimmy?" the voice said.

Jupe slammed down the receiver. He should call Arseneaux. *No, he shouldn't. Not during Jeopardy.* He stared at the phone. For a moment, Jupe thought he recognized the voice. Something about it sounded soft—and *mean.*

Twelve

The El Dorado Trailer Court

Shelby stubbed out the cigarette in a black plastic ashtray she "borrowed" from *The Lounge by Maurice* and sipped some strong, black coffee. She slid off the counter, and her bare feet stuck to a sticky spot on the cold linoleum.

She checked her wristwatch for the time. It was almost eleven in the morning. Time to tune into another thrilling episode of *Hospital Daze*! She maneuvered through the pile of shoes and magazines to the sofa and punched the remote. *Just in time!* The music had already ended, and the show had begun.

Nurse Gloria appeared, looking trim and blond, and worried. *Oo-oh Gloria! What's wrong? Is your heart in trouble?*

The dashing Gordon Fletcher, M.D. left a patient's room, after performing miraculous cures on a host of vague complaints, including, but not limited to, an ingrown toe nail, swimmer's ear, and two spider bites. While he was there, he examined the patient's spleen, and prescribed a ChapStick.

Shelby moved closer to the television screen to inspect the doctor's new "look." Check out *Gordon's dye job—love it, love it, love it!* A new shade of expresso disguised the gray in his thick hair, while subtle gray strands highlighted the chiseled features of his strikingly handsome face. *How'd he do that? Maybe he used a paintbrush, or even a toothbrush!* Oooh, *Hospital Daze* was getting juicy.

"Time to update my patient's chart!" he said. For a moment,

he admired his reflection in a smudged wall mirror at the nurse's station. Of course, he didn't notice the swarm of eager young nurses jockeying for crumbs of his attention while he slaved; that would be unprofessional. And, if it was one thing that Gordon Fletcher, M.D. was not, why, it was…

"Gordon, it's you!" Gloria said. Breathless, her glossy lips parted, her cheeks flushed, and of course, she was conveniently speechless. The buttons on her white uniform looked as if they might burst at any second.

Shelby craved a cigarette, but she couldn't go back to the bedroom to grab her purse now—not now, when Gloria and Gordon are finally…

Gordon Fletcher, M.D. glanced up from his official chart and yawned. "Gloria, it's you! Again. I knew you couldn't stay away from me for long. Does this mean you'll see me tomorrow?"

The stupid telephone rang! *Who would call at a time like this? Well, she wouldn't answer it. She had to know if Gloria was going to seize the moment. C'mon Gloria, she muttered to the stale air. Dr. Fletcher even dyed his hair! What's one itty bitty afternoon?*

Gloria didn't hear her. She glanced over her shoulder at Gordon Fletcher, M.D.

"Someone heard us, Gordon," she said.

"It doesn't matter to me," Gordon said. "Once and for all, Gloria, you've got to decide what matters. Do you want to die knowing you could have had it all with me—and passed it up? Is that what you want, Gloria?"

Gloria wept her bitter tears of anguish. "No, no, that's not what I want, Gordon. I've wanted you since the day we met, and now that you've dyed your hair that delicious shade of chocolate, or is it expresso? Well, it doesn't matter, I've decided to—"

Over and over again, the phone jingled, screeching like a fire alarm. Shelby slammed the empty coffee mug on the end table and ran into the kitchen. *The damned kitchen with the damned phone. Whoever was calling better have a good reason for this rude interruption. She'd been waiting for this moment since the first episode of Hospital Daze!* She reached the phone on the third ring. On the fourth, her cheeks flushed, her lips trembled, and suddenly, she was conveniently speechless.

"Shelby? Is that you?"

She knew the voice only too well. Now what could Elvin Suggs possibly want at a critical time like this? Obviously, he didn't watch *Hospital Daze*. Obviously, he hadn't discovered the medical world of Gordon Fletcher, M.D., or seen his new hair color.

"Yes, Elvin, it's me. I'm really busy right now and…"

"How 'bout I come over and take you out for a barbecue sandwich?"

"Look, Elvin, I'm watching *Hospital Daze*. So, I'm sure you'll understand why I can't leave this instant. I swear, Gloria and Gordon are sooo close to getting together, it's any second now, and that means I have to go, really, but I can see you in about an hour. 'kay?"

"*Hospital Daze*? You know, someone else I know likes to watch that show."

"Yeah, I do too." She punched a button to end the call and sighed.

Uh-oh, Gloria was back on the television screen, and…how could this happen again? Gordon Fletcher, M.D. sped away in his new red Porsche, with Nurse Gloria in hot pursuit, tears of regret spilling down her cheeks. *That nurse had to be blind. Gordon Fletcher, M.D. was gorgeous!* Without a doubt, Shelby knew that if she met anyone as exciting as Dr. Fletcher, she wouldn't be as silly as Nurse Gloria. *She would know a good man when she saw one.*

Bette's Barbeque
The same day, around 11:30 a.m.

Elvin pulled into the parking lot and breathed a deep sigh. "Vanna, this place brings back memories. Yep, it shorely does." Elvin recalled better days, when he and Cherie jumped into this same car, and pulled into this same lot. Grabbed some Memphis barbeque sandwiches and beer, and headed on back home. One night, they even ended up at the Scotland Yard Inn. Even now, he couldn't explain exactly how that happened. One thing, however, he recalled with utter clarity.

When they were together, Cherie had a way of making him forget anything and everybody. His eyes grew misty. Sakes alive, he missed her! Even after all that happened between them, Cherie's memory ignited a flame among the dying embers in his past. At the sight of her master's tears, Vanna began to whimper and whine.

"Sorry about that, Vanna. I shouldn't make you cry, too. How 'bout a barbeque sandwich, huh? Wait a minute, girl. What's that you got in your teeth?"

The terrier gripped a pink clutch purse in her mouth, Streams of drool coated the slick vinyl. He could have sworn Vanna smiled back at him.

"Y'all carrying a purse now, are you? Give me that, girl." The terrier dropped it in the front seat and stared at him. Elvin unsnapped the top of the purse, and searched its jumbled contents. Amidst the gum wrappers and tubes of lip gloss, he discovered Shelby's Missouri driver's license—just before he found a Nevada license that belonged to a woman named Krystal Light. *Sakes alive!* Elvin found yet another driver's license, issued in Mexico. It supposedly belonged to a woman named Kimmy Cruz. *No matter which license he picked to look at, a woman who looked an awful lot like Shelby smiled back at him. Hmmm.*

"There's a lot of folks in here, Vanna. Where'd you find this?" He cracked the glove compartment and slid the purse inside, next to the cherry licorice. "Let's keep all the pinky red stuff together, girl. That way, we're organized. You know, kinda like Di." The terrier seemed to stop smiling. "Don't worry girl, she ain't nowhere around. I can feel it when she is, 'cause it always gets a bit chilly. Like on the phone last evening."

What to do? Elvin thought for a moment, and decided. "Maybe Shelby likes barbeque sandwiches too, Vanna." Vanna stared back at him, and for a moment, he thought he caught a glimmer of a smile. "Who knows? Maybe all of those other folks in that purse do, too. C'mon, let's get us a mess of this stuff and head on over to see Shelby. We'll see what we can find out."

The Heartbreak Hideaway, Beale Street

"I'm telling you Rusty, we're a sunk ship." Lurlene Tate resembled a teenager, with her ruddy face and ragged fingernails.

Since 1969, Lurlene and Rusty Tate owned The Heartbreak Hideaway on Beale Street. The couple made a lot of money, and lost even more. Now, bankruptcy loomed like a brooding vulture, waiting to pick the bare bones.

The couple slouched in the Front Office and slurped Pepsi from Dixie cups. Humid air fogged the windows while they mopped their faces with cheap paper napkins.

"Leenie, since we lost our singer, nothing's been the same. She looked like Dolly, sure enough, but she didn't have the moves down." Rusty paused and gazed into the distance. "At least, not the way Dolly did. You know what that means? If things don't get better around here, we might have to go back to poker night, just to keep the cash from drying up."

"All this depressing talk reminds me. Did you call that woman back? You know, the one that came by last night? She seemed nice to me."

"Who you talking about?"

"Said her name was Krystal. She said she could sing—and how 'bout this? She says she can dance too!"

"They all say that."

"No. She sounded like the real thing."

"What does that mean?"

"She sounded like a real entertainer. Said she came back home to visit her mama, and asked if we had any jobs."

"What did you tell her?"

"Well, I told her I'd call her after I talked to you, is what I said. But, the more I think about all of this, Leenie, if she does accept our offer, we don't have the money to pay her. We barely have enough to keep the lights on and buy enough donuts, pizza and beer to keep the customers happy."

"Rusty, I think the worst thing to do would be for us to curl up and die. We have to pick ourselves up and keep going." Lurlene gulped the rest of her Pepsi. "Let's call her, and set up an audition, or an interview, or…"

"Okay. But, how do we pay her?"

"Let's meet her first. If she doesn't look and sing good enough to pull in a Beale Street crowd, then we don't need to be talking paycheck."

"Okay. You gonna call her? Or, am I?"

"You do it. You're the talent scout." Rusty reached for the phone, but it rang before he could dial the number. He listened and said, "Check back tomorrow, sir. Thanks for calling, hear?"

"Who was that?"

"Don't know. Get this—he said he wants to see Krystal Light's show. Had kind of a Spanish accent or something."

"He said that? Huh. Maybe that means our entertainment's getting famous."

"I don't think that will ever happen, no matter what we do. Hey, did I tell you about the two guys came round looking for Kimmy Cruz?"

"Nope. I don't need that kind of mess. I got my own troubles to work out."

"Maybe. Anyways, what does it matter? Even if we had any, we don't owe anybody any information."

"They wanted to buy what we knew, Lurlene. They had cash, and lots of it."

"Why didn't you say so?"

"You just said you don't need that kind of mess."

"I don't. But, I do need cash. I need money more than I don't need a mess." Lurlene stopped talking for a moment and frowned.

"What is it, Leenie?"

"Those show folks never use their real names. I read that in the TV Guide someplace. I know I did."

"Yeah. So?"

"So what if Krystal Light isn't her real name?"

"What else would it be?"

Lurlene paused for a second. "What if, just what if, it was Kimmy Cruz?"

"That would be crazy, Lurlene. Listen to you. Just crazy!"

"How much would your friends pay to know that?"

"They aren't my friends. Whoever they were, they had a stack of cash as thick as a phone book. I thought something was wrong with my eyes."

"Your eyes are fine. It's your brain what's got me worried. Did you write down their phone number? Can you get them to come back here—maybe this week? Maybe even tonight?"

"We don't have anything booked yet, Leenie."

"That's gonna change."

"It is?"

"Rusty Tate, you're gonna call Krystal Light, or whoever she is, and make us some real money. We just have to hope those Mexicans show up with their phonebook full of cash."

"Don't get yourself all riled up now. I'll know her when I see her, my darling, sweetums, love of my life."

"Don't try to sweet talk me. I can't believe you let those guys get away. But, we'll get them back. All we need is Krystal Light. You know that's not her real name. Nobody walks around with a name like that. You remember what this woman looks like?"

"Oh yeah."

"Good. Now, just let me have a few minutes to myself while I turn on the TV. My show's already started."

"Not that danged *Hospital Daze* again. Why do you watch that, Lurlene? It's just somebody else's dirty laundry."

"Today's the day Gloria and Gordon are going to get together, Rusty. Got to be someday."

"Don't see why." Despite his arthritis, Rusty decided to take a walk and try to unwind before he called Krystal. Personally, he didn't care if Gloria ever got together with Gordon. From what he saw at the Hideaway, such goings on caused nothing but trouble, man. Nothing but trouble.

Thirteen

The Eldorado Trailer Court, around noon

The announcer's voice boomed. "Keep your dentures white, right, and tight with GUMZ, the proud sponsor of Hospital Daze, the original reality show. This is the show that tells it like it is, folks. And now, stay tuned for another gripping episode of Hospital Daze!"

Shelby always felt a tiny chill when the announcer shouted those words. The episodes really were thrilling—the clothes, the makeup, the angst, the makeup, the clothes. She could go on forever, but there he was, Gordon Fletcher, M.D., large as life in his candy apple red Porsche. She leaned in to check out his hair color. He colored it again! *What would Gloria think of that? Would she notice?*

There was Gloria and, uh-oh, she'd changed her hair color too. *What would Gordon think of that? Would he dump her? Oo-oh, Gordon's talking now. Better concentrate on the snappy dialogue.*

"Gloria," Gordon said, "there's something different about you today. You're not looking well. Are you ill, darling?"

Is Gloria sick? Oh no!

"No, I'm feeling wonderful, Gordon. I love your new hair color. You look even better, and I swear, even more intelligent than before..."

"Not possible. But, yes, Gloria, you're right. I'm all about change. In fact, I was thinking that a change might be good for us."

Shelby fought her brimming tears. *How could Gordon Fletcher, M.D. be so callous?* He'd even told Gloria that her hair color made her look sick; at least, that's what Shelby thought he said. She wasn't quite certain of this, though. Apparently, neither was Gloria.

"But Gordon, you don't mean—you couldn't mean—a *separation*?"

"Only until you regain your health, Gloria. I'm quite certain that you're ill, darling."

"No, no, *no*, Gordon. It's just my new hair color. I'll change it if you don't like it. I'll change anything you don't like, no matter what it is. I need you now more than ever, Gordon. Please! Don't leave me alone now…oh Gordon, is there someone else?"

Violin music swelled. Gloria's anguished face melted into the shadows, just as the oversized pink box of denture adhesive spun and danced onto the television screen. The announcer's voice boomed. "And now, a word from our sponsor. You need 'em, we got 'em, so get 'em today, folks—GUMZ."

Shelby could not believe that the people at GUMZ wanted to say anything at a time like this. *Didn't they want to know everything, absolutely everything, about Gordon Fletcher, M.D.?*

Only seconds ago, Gordon Fletcher, M.D. suggested a separation. If GUMZ hadn't interrupted the show, she would already know by now if Gordon was in hot pursuit of another young vixen. Or not. Now, she would have to wait until tomorrow to find out! This always happened, and every time it did, Shelby swore she would stop watching the show. She was on the verge of doing just that when… *Who was pounding on the door like that?*

Shelby tightened the sash on her slinky kimono and tiptoed to the door. "Who's there?"

"It's Elvin!"

Elvin. Suggs? *Oh no. The guy with the dog.*

"Shelby, it's Elvin Suggs! I hope you like barbeque sandwiches, 'cause me and Vanna got us a carload full of them. Hey, open up and see for yourself."

Did Elvin say something about barbeque sandwiches? Shelby

thought she heard the magic words. She loved barbeque sandwiches, especially if they were from Bette's place over on LaMar Blvd. Well, it wouldn't hurt to eat a little barbeque with Elvin before she told him she had an audition for that job over on Beale Street at four o'clock, so...

She twisted the creaky knob and yanked on the door.

"Girl, what a beautiful sight you are!" Elvin said.

The air outside smelled so fresh, and yet, a smoky scent wafted into the dim trailer. Shelby stared at the man on the steps, laden with white paper bags and a six-pack of beer. There in the sunlight, Shelby thought he was a good-looking man. Better looking than she thought last night, in fact. His dog, Vicky, looked even messier.

"Thought we'd bring you a little lunch. Or might this be your breakfast?"

Elvin Suggs was like no other man she ever met. He seemed so simple, and yet, something told her he was anything but what he seemed. Right now, she felt hungry. She'd think about her thoughts later. "C'mon in, Elvin Suggs. You're making me miss my show. C'mon in. I guess Vicki can come in, too."

Elvin stared at her for a moment. "Thank you kindly, ma'am. She wouldn't understand any other way, I'm afraid. Besides that, I got all these sandwiches."

"Just set them down on the coffee table there, Elvin. *Hospital Daze* is getting ready to start up again. Oo–oh, there it is now."

"Get yourself some hot sauce on the top, Shel," Elvin said. He glanced at the television screen. "Hey, I know these folks. That's Gloria and Gordon, am I right?"

Shelby's mouth was full, and she finished chewing before she answered. "You're good. Most men don't know about *Hospital Daze*. But, I tell you Elvin, I'm getting really tired of waiting for Gordon and Gloria to get together, aren't you?"

Elvin felt entranced by this woman's beauty. So enthralled, he could barely talk, but somewhere inside, Elvin found the restraint he needed at the moment. "You need to follow a new show." He snatched the remote from her fingers and switched the channel. "Here it comes right now. Are you lucky or what?"

Rad World blared from the television so loudly, it seemed to vibrate. A close up shot of a sprawling medical center appeared on the screen, followed by a devilishly handsome radiologist, Dr. Rod Shocklee. "He's the guy always got himself in a fine mess," Elvin said. "My friend Di, she don't like him none."

"Who's that lady?" Shelby pointed to the photo of a bleached blonde in a scrub suit. She held a scalpel as if it were a demo item.

Elvin leaned closer to the television. "That 'lil gal? She's Rominia Rumiñez, the new surgery resident."

"Shh," Shelby said. "This show is really getting good." She crammed some coleslaw onto the oversized bun, and took another bite of her sandwich. "Is that woman a doctor too?"

"Shore 'nuf." Elvin bit into his sandwich and focused on the television screen.

"Rominia, where have you been all of my life?" Rod said. "I've never felt this way about anyone, I swear. Forget your career! Let's have a baby."

"But Rod, you already have a family. What will your wife say?" Rominia said. "Besides, my career will always come first."

"Then, you don't love me?"

"Of course I love you, Rod! Who wouldn't love such an intelligent, handsome, witty and sophisticated—"

"You can stop, Rominia. The list is endless, I know."

"Elvin," Shelby said, "this show is really good. So much conflict!" Elvin grinned. "I thought you'd like it."

Rominia began to tremble and sob, sob and tremble. "But Rod, I just want to have it all, and it seems so impossible! How can I have a demanding career with a sixty plus hour work week, a perfect husband, and of course, a show stopping family with—exactly how many more children do you want, Rod?"

"Well, right now, I only have seven. I was thinking that eight more would make a nice, round number, don't you think?" Rod said. "Fifteen sounds about right to me."

"Wow," Elvin said, "I didn't know old Rod wanted fifteen kids. That's a lot of…well, a lot of everything I can dang near think of."

Shelby rose and began to adjust the antenna. "There's something wrong with the sound on this television. For a minute, I thought that man said he wanted fifteen kids."

"Maybe he did." Elvin wiped the barbecue sauce from Vanna's beard. "The thing is, everyone thinks fifteen sounds like a crowd, but if it's one thing Dr. Rod loves, it's a big ole audience. I've been watching this show long enough to know that."

The theme music swelled and the announcer, well, announced. "Will Rominia consider Rod's proposal? Will she abandon her hard won, illustrious surgical career? Is Dr. Rod handsome, witty and intelligent enough for the ambitious Rominia? And, the Big Question, The One on everyone's mind: where is Rod's wife? Look for the answers to these and other pressing questions when you tune in to the next nail-biting episode of *Rad World*."

"Wow Elvin, *Rad World* is amazing! I need to thank you. If you hadn't come over when you did, I'd still be watching *Hospital Daze*. But, I'd better start cleaning up now."

"Why are you in such an all fired hurry, gal?" Elvin said. Shelby scurried around the sofa and coffee table, collecting bags and paper wrappers. He patted the sofa cushion beside him. "I thought we might visit a bit, you know."

"Well, you're not going to believe this, Elvin, but I got myself a job audition down on Beale Street, singing country music. It's something I always wanted to do."

"Beale Street? You must be a pretty good singer." He leaned back into the cushions of the sofa. He rose and opened the door of the trailer. "Go on outside for awhile, Vanna girl. Go on." The terrier refused to budge, but Elvin didn't seem to notice. "I had no idea I was talking to a star."

"That's what I'm trying to be. I even wrote a couple of songs."

"I think that's great. Well then, I could stay and go on down to Beale Street with you, or I could leave you alone to get ready for your big tryout. I'll do whatever you want me to do."

All at once, Elvin sensed a rising tension between them.

Both awkward and wonderful, the feeling crackled and spit like logs on a raging fire. Vanna barked, and again, he opened the door of the trailer. "Go on outside for awhile. Go on." He escorted the dog outside to the grassy area that surrounded the trailer. When he returned, however, Shelby was nowhere in sight.

"Shel, where'd you go?" Elvin rustled around the kitchen and living room. The ticking battery clock punctuated his every move. When he turned to leave, a slight rustle stopped him. The bedroom door creaked open, ever so slightly. He could barely see Shelby's face in the shadows.

"Elvin," she said, "would you like to come in here?"

Vanna's snores echoed through the open window. The afternoon breeze smelled warm and sweet. Somewhere, he heard a bird chirp. To be sure, Elvin felt light–headed, even dizzy. Still, he knew he didn't want to leave.

What he had with Cherie—those feelings he thought he'd never feel again—well, at this moment, he felt all of them. Wait. Could his heart survive another ride on the stormy sea of love: the questions with no answers, the locks without keys, and, most of all, the broken promises?

His brain didn't stop to ask those crazy questions, because his heart already knew the answers. The door opened wide.

Elvin gasped.

"Are you coming, boy?" Shelby said. "Or do I have to wait all danged day?"

Fourteen

Two hours later

A gentle rain sprinkled the roof of the trailer. Elvin awoke from a deep slumber, the likes of which he had never experienced. The spot beside him in the rumpled bed was empty. In the bathroom, water pattered on a vinyl shower curtain.

What did all of this mean? Elvin didn't exactly know, but right now, he did know that an undeniable sensation overwhelmed him. Sometime in the past two hours, a phoenix rose from the ashes of his grief. That pain that gnawed at his gut all the time, the hunger he never seemed to satiate, even with all the beer he drank with Cobra sometimes—all of it was gone. Elvin found the guy he hadn't been since Cherie left him. Turns out, that guy never left; and now, he felt a surge of strength that he thought had died. He never thought he'd feel this alive again.

He sat on the edge of the mattress and rubbed the back of his neck. It felt a little sore. Actually, it felt wet. He stared at his hand. Scarlet blood coated his fingertips. *What in the…*

He stood in front of the mirror and examined his neck. He didn't remember feeling any pain, but clearly, he had been bitten. *What else didn't he recall?* The sound of a voice in the distance startled him.

"Puddin! You come home to Mama?" Elvin heard the front door open, followed by the sound of a shrill voice. An image of Ethel Merman appeared in his head. Any minute now, he expected a full rendition of "Everything's Coming Up Roses." But, Ethel was dead, so who…

A bright red head of hair wearing the biggest pair of sunglasses in Tennessee and a bowling shirt with "Momma" embroidered on the left breast pocket appeared in the doorway. Elvin grabbed the sheet and snapped it under his chin.

"Well, lookee what Santy Claus brought me," Miss Red Hair said. "Don't suppose you know where I might find Shelby. Or do you?" She removed her sunglasses, and once again, Elvin gasped. A long, raised scar ran the length of one eye, and appeared to be permanently shut. "Oops, should have warned you. It's about my eye, ain't it?"

"No ma'am, I just wasn't expecting…"

"What? What weren't you expecting?"

Shelby appeared in the doorway. "Mama!"

"My baby girl! Who's the hunkster, baby? You done brought Elvis back to life, I do believe." Mama winked at Elvin. "But you know what? Before we ask him to take us out on the town, I think we're gonna go into the next room and let Elvis here get hisself all cleaned up."

"Shore 'nuf, Momma," Elvin said. "I'd be glad to take you out on the town."

"Well first, you're going to have to take care of that love bite there on the back of your neck, baby," Mama said. "You been at it again, Shelby Lynn? Looks like it hurts. Does it?"

"Mama, be nice to the company." Shelby twirled her hair with one finger while she spoke. "Besides that, I got something to tell you. I got me a job interview. Well no, it's really more of an audition."

"Yeah, what time is that, Shelby?" Elvin said. "I'd like to get a fresh change of clothes if we're going to Beale Street."

"As fast as you can get cleaned up and get back over here, Suggs," Shelby said. She winked at him. "You done had your audition, baby."

Elvin drove a little slower than usual on his way back to Newell Street. At his request, Vanna sat in the passenger seat, and helped him think. In all the years he was married to Cherie, he never experienced a bite like the one he received today. He didn't recall any pain when Shelby bit him, nor did he feel any now.

Again, he checked the mirror. *Sakes alive, that mess looks bad.* He felt so confused. Now, even when he felt bad, he felt good. How was he going to hide all of that stuff on his neck? He wasn't even sure he wanted to conceal it.

Elvin almost didn't see it. The stop sign seemed to grow straight out of the grass. He jammed the brakes fast and hard. The glove compartment popped open, and the contents, including the pink clutch purse, tumbled onto the floor of the Caddy. He opened it, and picked the Mexican driver's license from among the clutter. Elvin studied the photo of "Kimmy Cruz." Sure looked like Shelby Swain to him.

After he got cleaned up, he decided, he would return to Shelby's trailer. He needed to talk to Shelby or Kimmy, whoever she was. Krystal Light could come to the party too.

Fifteen

The Lounge by Maurice

"You've got to be kidding me." Reggie stared at the battered front door, illuminated by a single blue bulb. "You're telling me Shelby worked here?"

Myles sighed and turned his head. "When that woman got something into her head, there was no changing her mind, Reg. But, right now, I'm just trying to find her. I hope she's alright." He rested his head in his hands. "If only things had worked out between us."

"That's enough of that talk. No use in hashing the past, LaMour. And, I do know what I'm talking about. Believe it or not, I've got plenty of regrets I could cry about, but why? Today is almost tomorrow. So, put a lid on your pity party. Let's go."

Myles had to admit, Reg was probably right. Still, he couldn't help but blame himself for at least a part of Shelby's disappearance. He should have seen it coming, or he should have done something, he…

"Are you coming or not?" Reggie stood on the sidewalk beneath the barren trees, the bitter wind howling through the naked branches.

"Sure, yeah. Be right there." His cell phone rang; it was a call from Jupe. Should he pick up? He bit his lip and pressed the button marked *Answer*.

"LaMour?" Jupe's voice sounded raspy, strained.

"Yes Mr. Jupiter, good to hear from you."

"We need to talk. Now."

"I'll call you back."

"No, LaMour."

Myles clicked *End* and shoved the phone in his pocket. One problem at a time, he repeated to himself. *One problem at a time.*

"What took you so long?" Reggie said.

"Had to take a phone call. No big deal."

"Yeah. Okay. So, you want to do the talking, or should I?"

Myles shrugged. "I can if you want."

"You sure you're okay? You look a little rattled, my friend."

"I'm good."

The door opened, and Maurice White appeared, beer bottle in one hand and a cigar in his mouth. "Say, y'all look familiar." He chewed on the end of the cigar and peered into the shadows. "I b'lieve I know you from somewhere."

"You should," Myles said. "I used to come in at least three nights a week when Miss Shelby was on the stage. But now…well, I haven't talked to her in like, two, three days." He shook his head. "When's she coming back?"

"You know her, do you?"

"Let's just say I'm a fan."

"Huh. Woman has international appeal, she does." Maurice turned to Reggie. "What's up, Sarge? Somebody here get out of line?"

Reggie shivered. "Do you think we could talk inside, Mr. White? This won't take long, I promise you that."

Maurice took a swig from the bottle and turned to open the weathered door. "Look at that moon, willya? Looks like it's wrapped in cotton candy, don't it?"

Myles stared at the murky sky. "Interesting you should mention cotton candy tonight, Maurice. That was Shelby's favorite thing—she'd eat it anytime she could get her hands on it."

Maurice stepped into the dim foyer and shut the massive door with a bang. "What is this fascination with Shelby? Or should I say, Krystal Light?" Maurice chuckled. "Those Mexicans stuck to Krystal like wet bricks in fresh concrete."

"What two Mexicans you talking 'bout, Mo?" Reggie said.

"I figured you must a run into them somewhere, Reg. This town ain't that big and around here, they're like two chimps at a garden party."

Myles frowned. "What did you just say about a garden party?"

"I mean they don't look like they from St. Louis, you know?"

"Now, you really lost me," Myles said.

"For one thing, the one guy, you know the short, kinda heavy one, he's carrying this Colt .38 Super right out in front where everyone can see it. No one from around here carries a Colt .38 Super. That's a border thing. You know, they do that down around Texas."

"You know something, Moe," Reggie said, "I did hear something down at the station about two guys—Mexicans—just like you're describing there. But, till just now, I didn't make the connection. I mean, is there one?"

"I don't see one," Myles said.

"I do." Maurice shook his head. "Man, if I did something wrong..." He rubbed his neck and stared into the distance. "Jus' let me try and recall what they said. Besides Kimmy, they kept asking me about Shelby. I mean, I think they meant Shelby. They showed me a picture of a woman that looked jus' like her. But, they called her Krystal. Krystal Light. Around here, that was Shel's stage name. But, they also kept talking about someone named Kimmy. I don't know no one named Kimmy, Sarge. Do you?"

"Why is everything always so complicated?" Reggie said.

Again, Myles' phone rang. He glanced at it, and saw Jupe's name on the caller ID.

"I'd better take this. It's a client, calling for the second time in ten minutes, maybe less."

"Sure, don't mind us," Maurice said. "Get you a Coke or s omething, Sarge?"

"I'm fine," Reggie said. His eyes were fixed on Myles' expression.

"What's wrong, LaMour? You look sick to your stomach, if I can say that."

"That was Jupe on the phone, Reg."

"So? Did you tell him you were tied up?"

"Yeah," Maurice said. "Tied up, like Sarge said."

"You're shaking all over, LaMour," Reggie said. "What is it? What's wrong with Jupe now?"

"It's not Jupe I'm worried about." Myles locked his jaw for a moment and swallowed hard. "It's LaVerne."

"Mrs. Piece?" Maurice said. "Ask Jupe to look after her for a while till we're finished."

Myles wiped a tear from his cheek with the back of his hand. "That's exactly what he's been doing, Maurice." Again, he swallowed and then, cleared his throat. "LaVerne's dead."

Reggie stared back at him. "Who told you this?"

Myles glanced at Maurice, then back at Reggie. "I think I need to talk to my client."

Maurice chugged the last of the beer. "Sounds like it might be a little too late for that, LaMour." He turned to Reggie. "Lissen, I'll be here all night. If you want to go with LaMour here, why, I'm available if y'all need anything later on."

"Like what?" Myles said.

Maurice chuckled to himself and shook his head. "No telling," was all he said. He hustled down the hall and into the shadows.

"We'd better head over to the Galaxy. Want to ride with me?" Reggie said. "You look a little shook up."

"You keep on saying that. But, hey, this is a shock."

They drove in silence for the first few minutes. "Tell me, LaMour, how well did you know LaVerne?"

"Uh, well…"

"Okay, how long?"

"How long what?"

"How long did you know her?"

"I never said I did."

Reggie paused. The interview with LaVerne simmered on the back burner of his brain. "Well, did you?"

"What?"

"Know her?"

"I feel like I should have my attorney present."

"Funny, a guy like you talking like that." Reggie grinned. "Okay. No more questions." *For now, LaMour. At least, for now.*

Sixteen

Arseneaux's apartment
Around 7:00 p.m.

Nester grabbed a beer from the refrigerator and sank into
the lounge chair. He popped the can and gulped, the condensation
dripping between his bony fingers. "Ahhh," he said. "Now, where's that
remote control thing?"

The pounding on the door stunned him.

"It's time for *Jeopardy*, doesn't the world know when it's *Jeopardy*
time?" He punched the numbers into the remote. With every day that
passed, he was that much closer to his television debut, he…

"Arseneaux! Open up, it's Reggie!"

*Reggie? Like, The Sarg, Reggie? Like, Reggie, Your Parole Is Toast
Reggie?* Nester didn't want to take any chances. He cracked the door
and his worse fear stood in the hall. "Hi there, Sarg," he said. "Great to
see you. Like to watch a little *Jeopardy* with me?"

"I'm afraid the title of that show hits a little too close to home
tonight, Mr. Arseneaux," Reggie said.

"Yeah, and why is that?" Nester took another swig from the beer
can. "You mean you already know the answers to this part, is that what
you mean?" His eyes narrowed. "Hey, you're not thinking of being on
that show anytime soon, are you there, Sarg? 'Cause, I don't know if
you heard the news—or not—but yours truly is a *candidate*—I love
that word—for the championship. I kid you not one achy, breaky bit."

"Congratulations, Mr. Arseneaux. But no, that is not the reason for my visit here this evening."

Actually, Nester never believed it was. On the other hand, he could not imagine what dragged two guys like LaMour and Sarg here out in the cold and straight to his doorstep. "Right, there. So, what can I do for yous?"

"Have you seen Mr. Jupiter lately? Or heard from him? Any lead that you can provide will be helpful."

"You mean Jupe? Sure, I saw Jupe last night. He didn't have a place to stay, so I gave him the key to #207 so he could stay there, just overnight, you know. He's kind of hard up right now. He'll be moving out soon's as he gets some dough together. Don't worry, it's a temporary condition. Absolutely."

"You shouldn't have done that, Arseneaux," Myles said.

"We need to speak with him," Reggie said. "Immediately. Now, Mr. Arseneaux."

"Sure, go on up. I'm sure he's up there. Got no place to go, Jupe doesn't. He doesn't have any money to buy a ticket anywhere, that's how I know."

"That's interesting," Myles said.

"Want to come with us?" Reggie said.

"Well, I..."

"Mr. Arseneaux, we would really like it very much if you would accompany us to Apartment 207 to speak to Jupe."

"Okay, Sarg, *you* don't have to say it twice, there." *If Jupe scotched his parole, Nester would kill him. He would.* "Please allow me to set this beer down, there we go, and Nester Arseneaux here will be more than happy to escort yous upstairs to confer with the delightful Mr. Jupiter." *You have no idea how happy this makes me. No idea.*

Nester led the way up the gritty steps to the landing, now littered with cigarette butts. Reggie grabbed one of them and held it to the light of the bare bulb. "*Faros*, huh? Brand I've heard of, but never actually seen—before now." He pressed the used cigarette to his nose.

"Smells kind of sweet too."

"We don't allow smoking in here," Nester said. He pointed to the small sign, posted above the stairwell. With the "No" removed, it now said "Smoking."

"You going to fix that?" Reggie said.

"Next on my list," Nester said. He pointed to #207. "And as promised, here we are. New home for Mr. Jupiter." Nester pounded on the rickety door. "C'mon, Jupe, open up! *Jeopardy's* starting, I can hear the music already."

"Mr. Arseneaux, I..." Reggie began to advise the rotund man of his obligations as manager of the fine Galaxy on Grand Apartments, when Nester interrupted him.

"Say no more, Sarg. I keep my trusty key ring here for just these kind of no shows." *Last time he fronts Jupe an apartment, he swore to all the angels and saints, especially any and all who knew Jupe there.* He inserted the master key and jiggled the lock. It popped and the door sprung wide. "There we go, #207, for all the world to see. Now, if you two gentlemen will excuse me, I got a show to watch. And oh, stop by on your way out, hear?"

Myles nodded at Reggie. "After you, Reg."

Beale Street

"Where did you say this audition was, Shel?" Elvin said.

Shelby stared into the passenger mirror and applied her mascara, or rather, attempted to apply her mascara. Fascinated by the process, Vanna looked over her shoulder and panted. Her fuzzy image occupied at least half of the reflection. "Elvin, could you ask Vicki here to move to the right just a bit?"

Elvin chuckled. "That's the thing about staying so beautiful, ain't it? The makeup mirror is never big enough for two pretty girls. Right, Miss Vanna?"

"Your dog's name is Vanna? And all this time I've been calling her Vicki." She snapped her long finger. "So that's the reason she listens to you instead of me."

Elvin thought for a moment. "Maybe. Vanna's like a lot of ladies I know. Listens when she likes what she hears." He grinned like an impish schoolboy.

Shelby fluffed her platinum hair with her fingertips and sat up straight. "Well, what do you think?" She batted her eyelashes for emphasis.

"'Bout what?"

"Does this look professional? Do I look like the real thing?"

"Hmmm. A guy could get into a lot of trouble answering a question like the one you just asked me. Lemme just say here, Miss Shelby, I think you look like a professional entertainer. How'd I do?"

"That's exactly what I hoped you'd say."

"Dang! Never said the right thing before. That's what you do to me, I guess."

"Well, Elvin, I guess right now I need to find a new place called the Heartbreak Hideaway. 'Cause I have an audition or something like it in less than ten minutes." She rooted in the bottom of her purse for a scrap of paper, and finally, offered it to Elvin. "It's on Beale Street somewhere."

Elvin pointed to his right. "Well, all of this, as I suppose you already know, is Beale Street." He frowned and examined the rows of storefronts, concealed by the throngs of tourists and music lovers in search of evening entertainment. He took a few more steps and stopped in front of a two-story structure with a red heart on the front door. "This here used to be the Heartbreak Hotel, if I'm not mistaken. Got a different name, but it's still a vile shade of pink. Grainy like."

"You mean it's stucco?"

"Stuck where?"

"Stucco. It's a plaster finish."

"If you're going to get fancy on me now, I don't rightly know.

Vanna can stay with Arlo while we go inside. He owns a souvenir shop over on Beale. I really think I oughtta go with you. You never know what might be waiting on the other side of a door like that one."

"She won't mind?"

"Ma'am?"

"Vicki won't mind staying with Arlo?"

"Oh no. She likes to look at his postcard rack, especially the cards with the dogs on them. Sometimes, he lets her lick stamps, if someone wants to send one out right then. Makes her feel like she's a part of things. Besides, as long as we remember our manners and bring her a present when we come back, she'll be fine."

"What should we bring?"

"Oh, the usual. A rack of ribs usually works. Right, Vicki?"

"I didn't know a dog could laugh like that, Elvin."

"Oh, she's just smiling," Elvin said.

Shelby didn't reply. She didn't want to tell Elvin what she was really thinking: about how she didn't know a dog could act smarter than his owner—until now.

Seventeen

The Galaxy Apartments, #207

Reggie stood in the living room and studied the bloodstains, matted and brown on the snow white carpet. Myles preferred to poke around a bit, especially since it didn't seem like Jupe was presently at home. His sharp eye focused on a shell casing, balanced on the edge of a brass container that contained a potted plant. Like calipers, his fingers snagged it, and placed it in Reggie's outstretched hand for closer scrutiny.

"Don't see these much in St. Louis," Reggie said. "Or north of Texas, for that matter. This belongs to a .38 Super pistol."

"What are you trying to say?"

"I'm not trying to say anything. I just said it. Let me hold onto that while you find your client."

"He doesn't appear to be at home."

"No, he doesn't." Reggie stared at the bloodstained kitchen wall, sprayed in some macabre design. *Things were not adding up.* He took a deep breath and sighed. *Business as usual.*

Myles continued to proceed down the carpeted hall. *At least the carpet in here isn't stained.* Now, he stood at the end of the hall and faced a closed door. Maybe Jupe was asleep. Well, as his attorney, he would have to awaken him. Myles knocked on the door.

"LaMour, what are you doing?" Reggie stood behind him. "Just open the door. If Jupiter was here, don't you think he would have announced himself by now?" Reggie turned the knob and pushed.

The door banged against the plaster wall. Bright moonlight streamed into the room. "Aggh," Myles said, and covered his mouth with his hand. Reggie approached the far corner of the room slowly, yet deliberately. Who or what was that mound huddled in the corner? Each step brought him closer to the truth.

Propped against the wall, the woman appeared to be asleep. Her head rested on her shoulder, and her limp legs looked like they belonged to a rag doll, But Reggie knew the Big Sleep when he saw it— the final slumber from which no one awoke. The blood that dripped from her mouth, like the sticky blood pooled beneath her body, told him so.

"Where's your client, LaMour?"

"I don't know. Arseneaux told me that Jupe would be here." Jupe's voice echoed in his ears while Myles recalled his frantic phone call. *Should he mention it?* One look at the body in the corner and he decided. Not yet.

"Unless he resembles LaVerne Piece," Reggie said, "he's not here."

"Then, he's not here."

"And why isn't he, LaMour? Why would he leave? Or should I be asking why he would murder LaVerne Piece?"

"Wait just a minute. You have absolutely no proof or evidence to suggest Jupe murdered anybody."

"Why else would he leave the scene?"

"Who said he did that?"

Reggie glanced around the room and nodded his head. "I don't think anyone needs to say anything, LaMour. The problem is what's not being said." He flipped the light switch and further illuminated the garish scene. "And, a problem it certainly is."

"Maybe Arseneaux knows something about this."

"I suppose anything is possible."

"Well, I believe with all my heart that it's time to ask him."

"After you."

Myles stepped aside to allow Reggie the space to pass him in the long hall. "No, after you. I remember what happened the last time you said that to me. And, it's not going to happen again."

Arseneaux's apartment

The bells dinged while Nester drained his beer can and shouted to the television. "What is *Jeopardy*?" he said, over and over again. *How could anyone be so lame-brained? The answer, or rather the question, was as plain as the salt on his pretzel.* He took a whopping bite and began to munch the crunch, just as the pounding on the door grew louder, louder, and still louder.

"Yeah, Nester's a coming." He hoisted his lumpy body from the lounger and ambled his way to the door. One good yank and he found himself face to face with a detective and an attorney. *What is Jeopardy? The answer was as plain as the stripes on Reggie's suit. Look no further, my friends and fellow parolees. Nester Arseneaux is about to reup for the rest of his sorry life.*

"Mr. Arseneaux?" Reggie said.

"Mr. Arseneaux?" Myles said.

"You guys only need to ask me once," Nester said. "I am Mr. Arseneaux, times two, for your records there."

"When was the last time you saw or heard from Mr. Jupiter?" Reggie asked.

"I don't know any Mr. Jupiter."

"Let me rephrase the question," Myles said.

"Hey, do you like *Jeopardy*?" Nester said. "I think you'd be good."

"Let's stay on topic, Arseneaux. We need to find Jupe."

"I haven't seen Jupe since day before last. When he asked me for a place to stay. Hey, don't look at me like that. I'm not anything like either of you. I don't follow my people around—unless it's bug day. And, thank the moon and the stars, it's not bug day. Have you seen Jupe anywhere?"

"No, we haven't," Reggie said.

Myles remained silent.

"Well then, I guess we've got nothing to discuss. At least till he comes back."

"To the contrary, I'm afraid we do," Reggie said.

"Yeah, why is that?"

"When was the last time you saw Mrs. Piece, Arseneaux?"

"I thought you wanted to know about Jupe."

"We do. But, you didn't know anything about him. So, now we want to know about Mrs. Piece."

"What'd she do?"

"That's what we'd like to know."

"Huh?"

"Arseneaux, LaVerne Piece is in #207 right now."

"How'd she get in? She didn't have a key."

"That's what we'd like to know," Reggie said.

"You keep saying that. If you want to know how the lady managed to get into Jupe's apartment, then just ask her. It's that simple, gentlemen."

"No, Arseneaux, it isn't." Myles took a deep breath.

"I'm afraid you're going to have to come with us," Reggie said. "After you call an ambulance."

"What? But, I didn't... Take Mrs. Piece down to the station and make her talk, why don't you?" Nester grew quiet and stared at Reggie, then Myles. "Did you say ambulance? Did Mrs. Piece..."

"She's dead, Arseneaux," Reggie said. "Myles, you stay here and deal with the ambulance for Mrs. Piece. Arseneaux, grab your coat. We're going for a little ride."

Eighteen

Outside the Budget Motel

Cobra lit a cigarette and leaned against the Suburban. "Well, what did you think of the barbeque last night, Di?"

"That's the first time I ever ate spaghetti with barbequed pork in the sauce. Not sure I could duplicate it, but it was pretty good. I'm surprised Elvin hasn't tried that one on me, frankly. What did they call it?"

"Memphis Mac." Cobra blew a puff of smoke into the still night air. He stared at the stars and sighed. "Suggs hasn't answered my calls all day."

"I wish you hadn't said that."

"Want to look for his car or a different place to stay?"

Di stared back at him with the tenacity of a bulldog.

"That's what I thought," Cobra said. "Okay, so we're looking for a silver Caddy, and quite possibly a large Airedale. Am I right?"

"And a blonde with the eyes of an angel," Di said.

"Don't suppose they could be the same girl?"

"Not this time," Di said. "For once, I wish it was."

The Heartbreak Hideaway

"Pleased to meet you, Shelby, is it?" Elvin didn't care for this man who called himself Rusty, nor did he like Lurlene, his wife. Something about them smelled *faux*, a word Di used to describe fake stuff. Well, in Elvin's opinion, fake stuff described Rusty and Lurlene better than any two words alive.

"Shelby it is." The blond "angel" offered her manicured hand and Rusty squeezed it, then led her to the stage, comprised of a small platform linked to a short runway.

"Did you happen to bring any costumes?" Rusty said.

"Costumes?"

"Well, yes. You indicated you were a dancer."

"But, I hope to break into a country singing career. This is Memphis, after all."

Rusty and Lurlene exchanged a glance that Elvin didn't fully comprehend, yet he understood that he didn't like it. "Yes, well…" Rusty said. He stared at the floor.

Lurlene chimed in to cover the awkward interlude. "What Rusty is trying to say is that we've never really had a country singer perform live in here before—just dancers. But, we're entirely open to new ideas. To be completely honest with you, our little business here is trying to make a comeback, here in downtown Memphis. Whatever you do, do it well. Make us proud. That's all I ask."

"Okay, then. Want to hear what I can do?"

"Let's get down to it."

Elvin watched their faces melt while they listened to "Why Should I?" Shelby wrote the music and the words for the story of breakup and regret.

"I like it," Rusty said.

Shelby liked that remark. "Great."

"But, we'd really like to see you dance."

Lurlene nodded. "The girl we had before you danced. A lot."

"That wasn't what I had in mind. I wanted to focus on a singing career. Country music."

Elvin sensed the mounting tension. It was bigger than dancing, bigger than singing…hey, what pushed these folks' buttons? "Why can't Shelby do both?"

"And you are?" Rusty said.

"I'm Elvin Suggs, sir. I'm from around these parts."

"Really? Where did you live, Mr. Elvin?" Lurlene said.

"Newell Street. 936. Next door to Mrs. Chandler."

"I'll be. She died a while back, you know."

"No!"

"Oh yeah. But, we all do, Elvin."

"Leenie," Rusty said, "we got to make a decision here. It's getting to be time to open for the night."

"Would you excuse us for a lil' ole second?" Rusty rose and headed for the back room. "Leenie and I would like to briefly discuss a few things. We'll be right back."

Once they reached the dim corridor, Lurlene unleashed her frustration. "Why did you encourage that girl? We don't need or want a country singer. Are you crazy? I have enough applicants to last me for the next ten years. I might not survive to read all of them after the year we've just had. Rusty, are you listening?"

"Sure. I'm listening. But, there's something you need to know, Leenie."

"What?"

"I talked to those guys with the pile of cash today. You know, the ones with a roll as thick as a phonebook? The ones you asked me to get in touch with?"

"You found them?"

"Oh yeah, I found them alright. Or I should say, they found me. They said Arlo from the souvenir shop told them we were looking for a dancer. Guess what? They came in first thing this morning for a visit."

"What do they want?"

"They want Shelby. Or should I say, Krystal Light? She might even have another name she uses, I'm not sure about that. But, there's one thing I am sure of—she is very valuable to these guys. And, they have the cash to make it worth the hassle."

"Why do they want her so much?"

"No idea."

"What did you tell them?"

"I told them I'd make sure she was here when they were."

"Tonight?"

"Okay."

"Okay. Let's go back in there and tell her to start tonight. She can sing, dance, and smoke cigars if she wants to. I don't care what she does on that stage, so long as she stays around long enough for us to collect the *dinero*."

"The what?"

"The money! You know. The cash. Don't you understand plain English?"

Lurlene didn't answer. She knew there was no point to an argument with Rusty over plain English. Or singing or dancing. She would save her energy for the *dinero*.

Nineteen

Outside the Heartbreak Hideaway, Beale Street

"Call me crazy, Di, but doesn't that guy across the street look just like Elvin?"

"For starters, never let anyone tell you you're not crazy." She shielded her eyes from the late afternoon sun, or attempted to, while she searched for the subject of their discussion. "You definitely are. I cannot believe how hot it is in Memphis, even at this time of the day." Her eyes widened at the sight of the couple, now almost directly facing her.

"You know something, Mama? You're not looking so good around the gills." Cobra sucked a final drag from his cigarette and tossed the butt into a nearby sewer. "Don't look now, but it's Suggs and an angel. Should I holler or are you gonna cry first?"

"Go ahead."

"If I didn't know better, I'd think you were jealous." He paused and decided to stop doing whatever it was he was doing with Di's feelings, and direct his mischievous energy toward Elvin and the Angel. What a fine one she was, too. Kinda reminded him of Valerie in a way, except that no one ever called Val an angel. Nope, not even once. Ever.

"Hey, Suggs! Over here, Suggs!" he said and waved his arms above Di's long neck and auburn hair. "It's me, Suggs! Cobra!"

For a split second, Cobra thought Suggs planned to ignore them. Crazy, sure. But, his instincts were usually precise, and that's what they declared to his senses, loud and clear. But, in the end,

Suggs' effervescence seemed to conquer his pride, at least from where Cobra stood.

"Cobra! Di! Sakes alive!" Suggs said. "Come over and meet my new girl."

Cobra noticed how Suggs' words caused Di to flinch, particularly the reference to his "new girl." *Funny thing.* After hanging out with Di for the past few days, he was starting to get the hang of the whole woman's intuition thing. *Who knew where this new path might lead?* By the time they returned to St. Louis, he could even be ready to start reading some of those women's mags. Di especially liked the ones that talked about new relationship no no's and what to do about stuff like being ignored, and…

Nah, forget it. Just forget it.

Cobra nodded. "Hi," was all he could think to say, right before he added, "I'm Cobra." He noticed the way in which the two females regarded each other; kind of like two terriers sparring in a show ring at Westminster. But, he sensed—no, he *knew*—this would not be a great time to make such a comparison.

"Di," Suggs said, "this is Shelby."

In Cobra's estimation, Shelby seemed to attempt to hide behind Elvin. Well, even he could sense the tension between the two women. *Why did Di have that effect on other women?* It seemed to Cobra that she could see straight through another woman from the second that she met her. The most unnerving part was that she was usually right in her assessment. *Weird, man. Just plain weird.* And here she was, doing it again, whether she or Suggs realized it or not. That had to be the reason that Shelby here acted so skittish. Cobra actually felt sorry for her. Di could be pretty intimidating sometimes, she…

"Shelby, where you off to?" Elvin said.

Without a word, the blonde raced down the nearest alley, with Elvin in hot pursuit.

"They're in the back there. See them, Cobra?" Di said.

Elvin's voice echoed from the alley. "Run for the car, Shelby!"

Cobra saw two men with faces like concrete statues, one tall, one pudgy and short, worming their way through the crowd. *What had Suggs gotten himself into this time?* He inched his way through the milling crowd. He'd lost them. At least he thought so, until he heard the voice, spiked with the hot sauce of Southern pride.

"Pay for it, homey."

Cobra turned to see a short, olive–skinned man, restrained by the hands of a thick-boned, black man, possibly a foot taller, and certainly much angrier.

"What is *homey?*" Fear oozed from the short man's skin. At this point, he seemed to know that every breath he took was valuable. "Eduardo! 'Splain it to him."

Cobra figured Eduardo must be the tall, dark man who resembled a skinny gorilla. "*Sí.* We are on vacation."

"I don't care where you are. Your bro' here dumped my business, my barbecue and beer all over the damn sidewalk. That represents the masterpiece—you hear me, Gonzales?—the masterpiece I done been working on since dawn. So you tell me, what I'm gonna do to feed my kids now it's done time to sell what I don't have now, because your homeboy just went and dumped..." Here, he pounded Santy's back with his fist for emphasis. "I said, dumped my ribs with his self-important self. Man's got no respect for what's mine, running through the streets like a wild animal. Don't know where y'all be on vacation from, but down here, we don't appreciate no respect. So, what you gonna do about it? I can't hear you, Gonzales." The man glared at Eduardo and Santy like an angry bull ready to charge.

Cobra thought this might be a good time to leave, but hell, it was such a good show, he decided to stay, for just a few more seconds...

Eduardo stepped forward and flaunted a wad of cash that, at first, Cobra thought was a roll of toilet paper. He peeled off an impressive stack of C–notes and pressed them into the thick flesh of the man's hand. "*Muy contendo.*"

The man gawked at the money and his eyes widened. "I don't know what you just said, but I know what this cash here does. So, yeah, okay, *contendo* to you, too. An' let me give you a little tip, Gonzales. This is America, home of the free and the brave, the US of A. Either learn some better English—homestyle, hear? Or get yourself some faster running shoes. That's the best advice you're gonna get today in Memphis, Tennessee." The man stuffed the stack of bills into his thin wallet. "Y'all have yourselves a real fine–ass day today now, hear?"

Eduardo and Santy exchanged glances. "Is he insulting us, Eduardo? What kine of day we have?"

Eduardo studied the sky, now dotted with leaden clouds. Thunder clapped in the distance. "This must be what he call a fine–ass day, Santy. *Americanos.* They love to predict their weather." He shrugged. "No accounting for tase. Come, we will get us some of this barbeque."

"What about the Kimmy?"

Eduardo shrugged. "A man has to eat, Santy." He poked Santy's belly. "Eh?"

"*Sí, Señor.*" Santy smiled.

"She will be here."

"How do you know?"

"She must eat too. We will talk to Arturo later."

"Okay." So far, Eduardo had been right about everything. Besides, every mystery had a solution. There was a season for everything under the sun. *Sí* and *todas gracias.* Now, he would try some of this fine Memphis barbeque.

Twenty

"Follow me to Newell Street, Cobra," Elvin said. He silenced the cell phone and glanced in the rear view mirror at Vanna. "How you doing, girl?"

"You know, Elvin," Shelby said, "a real live girl is sitting up front right here next to you."

Elvin stared straight ahead when he spoke. "I'm getting to that part."

"What do you mean that part? What part?"

"Vanna looks like she's kinda of hungry. Sometimes, Arlo shares his donut with her, but lately, he's been on a diet. Why don't you open the glove box in front of you and get the candy out. She likes the cherry kind."

"Elvin, I…"

Elvin grinned. "She'd really appreciate the favor, Shel. So would I."

"All right." The pretty blonde with the manicured nails popped the lock on the box. Without warning, the contents spilled all over the seat, Shelby's lap and the floor of the Caddy. One item in particular caught her attention. She nabbed it with the speed of a Texas tornado, but her haste didn't escape Elvin's scrutiny. In fact, he anticipated precisely such a reaction.

"I was meaning to ask you 'bout that pink purse," he said. "You know, my late wife just loved sweet 'lil purses just like that."

Shelby glared at him with accusation in her eyes. He could tell she wondered where he was going with this monologue and wondered who or what was his destination. *Would she play along with him?*

"What's it doing in your glove box, Elvin? I've looked high and low for this purse and couldn't find it. Let me tell you, it's caused me a heap of trouble. I wished you told me you found it."

"Wasn't exactly sure who it belonged to, Shel. There's three driver's licenses in that purse. Couldn't hardly fit 'em all in, and one is from Mexico. Now, does that sound a little crazy to you?"

"It's my purse. I'm going to take it home tonight."

"If you're fixin' to do that, I believe I need to see some ID." The expression on Elvin's handsome face never changed. "Who are you today, Miss Shelby? Let's see now—just who am I talking to right now?" He grinned at her with a fresh energy. "What do you think, Vanna? Is it Shelby, or is it Kimmy or Krystal?"

The lady stared at Elvin with a fresh determination. "Elvin, what is wrong with you? I told you my name is Shelby, and it is."

"Who and where are those other gals?"

"Kimmy and Krystal are my stage names."

"Uh, uh," Elvin said. "Do they drive in Mexico while they're singing and dancing?"

Elvin turned into the driveway of the small house on Newell Street. "Here we are. Looks like we're the first to get here." He turned to the woman beside him, the one with the tears in her eyes. "You need to tell me the truth. Always. 'Cause I can't and won't love a woman I can't trust. Already done that." He snapped his fingers. "Say, maybe those Mexican guys are looking for your driver's license!"

Shelby stared at the small, neat bungalow that used to be Elvin's home. "Something like that."

"Well, they already have a good picture of you and all, so why don't you just up and let them have it? Surely you won't be needing it in Tennessee. Won't do you no good around here anyway."

"Elvin, have you ever done anything you never wanted anyone else to know about?"

Elvin paused and took a deep breath. "Okay. Sure. You want to talk about my time in 'Nam, is that it? Because yeah, I killed people I didn't want to kill when I was over there, people in the wrong place at the wrong time. People find out I was in 'Nam, they call me 'baby killer' and all kinds of other vile names. But, if I hadn't killed them first, I wouldn't be here right now, talking to you. I was living second to second, Shelby. Don't know if you can imagine that, but…"

Cobra tapped on the glass of the driver's window. "Open up, Suggs. We got some serious talking to do."

"That's just what Shelby and me were doing. She asked me if I ever did anything I didn't want anyone else to know about."

Cobra studied the blonde. "She did, huh? Well, Suggs has nothing on me in that department. Let's get inside and I'll tell you the good stuff."

Shelby smiled, but didn't speak. She didn't need to say a word. Elvin knew that smile. Same one that as his wife, Cherie, had, the woman who lived with him in the house he was about to reenter. He opened the car door and turned to face Cobra. He didn't like the expression on his face. He'd seen that before too, when Cobra was waiting to fire on his mark. He started for the front door and realized there was someone else he understood just as well, maybe even better. "Vanna! Come on, girl. We're home!"

Motel room, downtown Memphis

"*Sí*, Arturo, it is Eduardo. *Sí*. Santy is with me." Eduardo peeked at the name of the motel on a thin tablet of paper. "We are in a motel, Eet is called the Scotland Yards. *Sí*."

"You are in Scotland?" Arturo said.

"*Sí*, in the Scotland Yards. In Memphis. In Tennessee. We are everywhere!"

"Hmm. So, you got the Kimmy? You got my *dinero*. *Sí*?"

"We know where she is," Eduardo said. "We foun her last night."

"*Bueno*! So, put her on the telephone."

"A little problem, Arturo. The Kimmy, she is not with us. Santy, he have a problem with the barbecue guy, he—"

"Let me tell you something, Eduardo. Are you listening? And you can pass this on to Santos. I am not amused. You bring the Kimmy to me in twenny four hours or I will come to you. Now, my problem is your problem, Sí? Comprende?"

"But, Arturo…"

"I don't know how you take so long to fine one woman. What is wrong with you? And another thing. Both of you, get out of Scotland." The phone banged in Eduardo's ear.

Former Suggs home, Newell Street

The minute Elvin opened the front door, Vanna raced to the back of the bungalow.

"That dog looks like she knows the place by heart," Shelby said.

"Yep," Elvin said, "Vanna doesn't forget a thing." The corner of his eye crinkled in mock amusement. "I'm kinda like that sometimes."

Di and Cobra remained silent. From the corner of her eye, Di watched Elvin drop his keys on the sill of the wide front window. As if in slow motion, he moved through the small rooms, inhaling the stale air as if he could breathe a bit of Cherie back into his life. One glance at Shelby, and it almost looked to her like he had done just that. Except, there was something about Shelby that seemed more sophisticated, smarter, or maybe even tougher than Cherie; what it was, Di couldn't say—yet.

"Hey, Suggs, why don't we order a pizza? That way we can have something to eat while we talk about the two guys that chased Shelby down Beale Street." He nodded. "With all respect, ma'am, I would like to know what they wanted."

Di didn't take her eyes from Shelby's face: a face that smiled like a mannequin, with eyes like cold, blue marbles and hair like a Barbie doll. Cobra's question couldn't pierce the façade.

"Why, I have no idea," she said.

"You know how some men are about beautiful gals, Cobra," Elvin said. They see that blond hair and they just gotta chase it."

"Yeah Suggs, and why is that?"

"Why not?" Elvin stood in the middle of what used to be the master bedroom, and hummed an impromptu tune. Repeatedly, he opened and shut the closet doors, until he stopped and stared.

At that moment, Di strolled into the room.

"What is it, Suggs?" Cobra said.

The beefy man dug to the depths of the darkened space. He grabbed a small clutch purse, done in a shade of pink that could only be described as "Cherie Cotton Candy." Even as his mouth quivered, he struggled to smile.

"C'mon Shelby, I'll show you the kitchen," Cobra said. "There's nothing more to see here."

"But, Elvin might need me…"

Di turned and glared at Shelby with an expression that only another woman could decipher. "We'll meet you in the kitchen."

Cobra grinned. "You know, you remind me of someone else I know with that same color of hair. Ever hear of a gal named Valerie Gains?"

Even the mention of Valerie's name didn't matter to Di, compared to Elvin's emotional demise. His shoulders quivered with grief; the heat of his tears seemed to melt his body. As if it were a priceless relic, he raised the purse above his head. "Cherie's," was all he managed to say, before the torrent of his sobs overcame him.

Di tried to hug him, but he pushed her away. "I got to do this myself, Di. You don't know what we had together. I know you didn't like her, but I loved that woman. Would have done anything for her." His sobs echoed throughout the small home. Di was certain that Cobra and Shelby heard them.

"What's with the purse, El?"

Elvin turned to face her. Red patches and wet tears covered his cheeks. "What?"

"The purse. The sight of it set you off. Why?"

"I don't know. I can't answer that. It's just that until Shelby, I never knew anybody who carried a 'lil ole pink purse, not the way Cherie did. Only one gal like Cherie. I still love her. What am I going to do?"

Di sighed and stared at Elvin. "Don't you think I think of Don every day? What woman wouldn't? There won't ever be another one like him. But, that's the way it's supposed to be."

Elvin brushed a tear from his face. "What do you mean?"

"I mean, even if a man tried to imitate Don, he couldn't. Don was the original class act. He lives in a corner of my heart where no other man will ever go. But, that doesn't mean there isn't room in there for someone else who might come along. There is."

"What are you saying?"

"Elvin, I'm saying, let Cherie rest in peace. You don't have to forget her. But, you're still alive. The people you talk to should be, too. You might even like a few of them."

"You know, you almost talk like you liked Cherie too," Elvin said. "Deep down, I always thought you did." He stretched out his hand that held the pink purse in it. "Here. Why don't you take this? It would make me happy to know that you had Cherie on your mind sometimes too."

"It would?" Di stared at the purse as if it were a dead possum.

"Shore 'nuf. Here, go on, take it. Sakes alive, I do believe I feel much better." He mopped his forehead with a red bandana handkerchief.

Cobra appeared in the doorway. "That's good to hear, Suggs. Would you look at this? It's Di, with a pink purse." He tilted his head, first to the left then to the right. "You know, in this light, if you got yourself some real shiny lip gloss, and maybe a little bubble gum, and then spray that head with lots of hair goop, I'd—"

"Stop," Di said. "Just stop."

Elvin almost smiled. "It's going to take more than all a that trash to change a lady like Di. Anyway, I like her fine the way she is." Elvin stopped talking and craned his neck past Di's head into the hallway. "Where'd Shelby run off to?"

"What's that sound?" Di said.

"Sounds like a car in the driveway," Cobra said.

Elvin pushed past Di and Cobra, and rushed into the tiny living room, just in time to see the beam of headlights shining through the front window. One glance at the empty window sill answered their questions.

"There goes my car," Elvin said, "with Shelby in it."

Cobra grabbed the keys to the Suburban. "C'mon, we'll follow her."

"Why did she do that?" Elvin said. "I guess she done felt ignored."

"Where do you think she's going?"

"She's going back to her mama, shore 'nuf," Elvin said. "Back to The El Dorado Trailer Court."

"Why don't you call her cell phone?" Di said.

"That's a danged good idea. I'll do it now."

The *brrring* sounded, shore 'nuf, from the kitchen floor, where the phone had fallen.

Cobra picked it up and held it to his ear. "Leave a message for Kimmy or Krystal and Shelby will call you back," a voice said. He clicked the *Off* button and strolled into the living room. "Here's her phone, whoever she is, Suggs."

Di and Cobra exchanged glances. "Who's driving?" Di said.

"You are. I might have other things to watch besides the road. Suggs, get in the car. We're going for a ride."

Twenty One

About an hour later

Shelby checked the rear view mirror. Where she was headed, they'd never find her, especially if she ditched this crate of a car. Besides, it had dog toys and used blankets all over the backseat, not to mention that gigantic waterbowl. *Yuk.*

After almost twenty minutes and three left turns, the silver Caddy cruised along Lamar Avenue. One more turn, and there it was—Shelby's favorite hideout in Memphis, if she had one. Nowhere could a girl find a better One Star motel with a room for $39.95. She wondered how it came to be called the Scotland Yard Inn. After all her trysts here through the years, she wondered now why she wondered now.

The parking lot appeared nearly empty, except for another car parked in the rear of the building. She decided to park there too, next to a gold-tinted Mercury sedan. Beside the silver Caddy, the Mercury glimmered in the moonlight. Conspicuous, to be sure.

Shelby crept to the Front Office, where the light beamed below a neon sign that said, Yard. The word Scotland, for whatever reason, was burned out. By the time Shelby reached the front desk, she was too. Otherwise, she might have noticed the name of another customer on an invoice, the one that lay on the desk next to the cash register, and slipped under the door, of a room registered to *E. Ruiz.*

The El Dorado Trailer Court

In Gilda's mind, the best part about a show like *Rad World* was, if a person like her missed an episode, why, they could watch the rerun at 7:00 the following morning. Which is exactly what she planned to do, since she missed yesterday's shenanigans because of a shooting competition at the range, at which, by the way, she won first place.

Now, she intended to clean her gun and catch up with Rod and Rominia. The pungent odor of Hoppe's No. 9 solvent penetrated the air. Gilda turned up the sound. She couldn't believe her ears. Something must be wrong with the antenna again.

"Rod," Rominia said, "I don't believe it! You don't mean that. I know you don't!"

Gilda wondered what Rod didn't mean. She listened even closer.

"Yes, Rominia, I do," Rod said. "For me, some things are like butter on toast, like rain on the roses, like nails in a coffin…"

"Say that again?"

"I don't have the time to debate our differences, Rominia. Neither do you. I'm madly in love with you, but you must return to your gall bladder surgery."

"Oh, that's right! How could I forget?"

"The team is still waiting. That's something that I can't do. I need to know now if…"

The announcer's voice boomed. *And now, a word from our sponsor, EATITALL dog food.*

Gilda almost dropped her revolver. *What were those sponsors thinking?* This was not the time to interrupt a quality show like *Rad World* to advertise EATITALL dog food. Not that she knew much about a dog food like EATITALL, not having a dog and all… Now, what was that noise? She rose from the kitchen table and tottered over to the sink. Bright light beamed through the window above it.

Gilda peered into the shadows of the dawn, and saw an older gray Suburban. Though the vehicle was unfamiliar, someone in it was not.

She'd never forget the man that emerged from the backseat. What was his name? Didn't matter. She ran a comb through her hair and smeared some lipstick on her crinkled lips. *Now, to the door.* She opened it and smiled at the hunk of man that grinned back at her.

"Good morning, ma'am," Elvin said. "Hope I didn't disturb you."

"Kind of early for you to be visiting, isn't it?" Gilda said. "Is Shelby with you?" The old woman scanned the gravel driveway behind him and frowned. "Maybe she already ran into the house."

"Ma'am?"

"Oh, she called me a little while ago and asked if her Mama was home. But, you know Letha. Or, maybe you don't." Gilda chuckled. "Sometimes, I don't know if any of us knows Letha. Anyway, Letha's over at the boat again, playing the slots. When she goes over there for the night, I usually don't see her for oh, a couple a days. At least."

"Is that all she said?"

"Well, no. I wonder if you know anything about this." Gilda looked off into the distance. "My, what a pretty sunrise. Well, she asked me if I still had a spare gun or two she could buy from me." Gilda looked at her feet. "You know anything about that?"

Elvin hesitated. "No, can't say as I do. Did she say anything else?"

"Just that she was on her way. Why don't you come on in and have a cup of coffee with me? Maybe some biscuits? I make a mean biscuit, Elvin." Gilda smiled and, for a fleeting moment, a girl emerged from beneath the wrinkles and lines in the sagging face; the woman that once was the age Elvin was right now.

"Oh man, does that sound fine," he said. "But, you know, I got my friends waiting in the car. And, my girl, Vanna."

"Well," Gilda said, "Shelby would never forgive me if she thought I was entertaining her boyfriend's girlfriend. So, y'all better wait in the car till she shows up."

"Oh, I can explain about Vanna."

"I'll bet you can. Better save it for Shelby. You know, I didn't have you figured for a playboy." The thin door slammed shut. Elvin tiptoed down the steps to the car and cracked the door.

"What'd you find out, Suggs?" Cobra said.

"We'll wait right here," he said. Vanna stared at him with adoration in her black eyes. "Hey there, girlfriend. Did you know you're sitting next to a playboy?"

Di turned and gave them a withering glance. "It wouldn't matter what you were, Elvin. She'd sit there forever, and look at you like you were the best thing she ever saw."

"Yeah." The sun rose above the purple haze and Elvin sighed. Wished he could find a woman who acted like that.

Did she exist? If she did, was she looking for a man like him? He smiled at Vanna and ran his hand over her wiry coat. Well, if a woman like Vanna was looking for him, he hoped she didn't drool on the backseat.

7:15 a.m., the same morning

"Don't call me with this stuff no more, Jupe, you hear me?" Nester hustled aroud his bedroom, struggling to dress while he conversed. "Why didn't you tell me you and Miss LaVerne were married? Yeah, for the love of gravy, it was me that found the divorce papers. They were in LaVerne's jewelry box, locked up and all for Chrissakes." He pulled on a black sock, then a navy blue one. "I don't care if it was for two hours, you two were husband and wife. No, I don't want to know why. And no, I don't believe you wouldn't kill her for any amount of money. C'mon, Jupe. This is me you're talking to."

Nester glanced at the alarm clock on the cluttered dresser. At the mention of their mutual acquaintance, the furrows on his brow deepened. "I need to tell you, Jupe, LaMour is no fool. He's on to you in a big way. Now that I think about it, he probably knows more about you than I do." He grabbed a tweed jacket from the closet and slipped it over one arm, then another. "And, I know a lot." He shook his head. "I told you from the start, Jupe. Nothing, and I mean nothing, is going to stand in the way of my freedom. I have sixty–two days remaining, counting today. I am, in fact, on my way to see my parole officer as we speak. After that, I'm dropping my application for the *Jeopardy* show in the U.S. of A. mail. My big chance. I am not gonna blow this for you or anyone else."

Nester hung up the receiver and wiped his brow. The nerve of a guy like Jupe, wanting him to get involved, throwing out alibis for him. Sure, Jupe was a friend, and friends were like gold in this world, didn't he know that better than anyone? He wouldn't be on the street right now without Jupe's contacts and LaMour's smarts. But, truth was, he didn't know where Jupe was when Miss LaVerne died. And, the big one—he didn't know they were once husband and wife. Never would have put that one together, not in a million. Which made him wonder: what else had he missed? A knock on the door interrupted his musings. He opened it to find Reggie standing in the hall.

"Mr. Arseneaux," he said. "So good to find you at home. May I come in? Just a few questions, about Mrs. Piece, upstairs."

Uh-oh. Sounded an awful lot like *Jeopardy* to him.

Twenty Two

Jupe didn't feel good about this one. For one thing, he didn't like the morning deals—in his experience, cops were always around in the early hours, fresh as new mown grass. Something else bothered him. When Shelby called, the edge in her voice could slice sandpaper. Jupe's impressive rap sheet taught him to pay attention to little things; details, like time and tone. In the end, he found that those little things added up to a big thing that nearly ended his short-lived career. He wouldn't let that happen again. He couldn't afford another mistake.

So, he asked himself, why was he driving to the outskirts of Memphis, to a one star motel? Maybe he wanted to see Shelby—what guy wouldn't? Maybe he wanted to make a score. He could always use the cash. But mostly, yeah, he liked the smell of risk, the thrill of the chase, and the rush of victory that always accompanied a pursuit.

A new feeling disturbed him. This time, success didn't feel inevitable. Jupe gave it a fifty–fifty chance. With odds like that, failure seemed just as likely. He parked the car by a chain link fence at the far end of the lot. Just because failure seemed likely didn't mean it would happen.

Shelby told him to look for a silver Caddy. His grimy hands shielded his eyes, while he studied the parking lot. Except for the two cars with dealer's plates, the space looked empty and deserted. Well, no one seemed to care what vehicles were or weren't on the lot. He crept closer to the cars and waited.

Scotland Yard, Eduardo and Santy's Room

"*Amigo*," Eduardo said, "what are you looking for?" The skinny man snickered. "A phonebook or somethin'? Maybe you think you gonna give the Kimmy a wake up call, eh?" He sat on the sagging mattress, and reached for his pack of cigarettes.

"I am looking for a room service menu. This is America, Eduardo. Anything is possible."

"This room," Eduardo said, and gestured to the modest decor around him, "is ours, Santy, for the total price of $39.95. Now, I remember! I think—here," he paused and narrowed his beady eyes— "if I am no mistaken, there is free breakfast. What time is it?"

"You're always asking me the time. 'What time is it, Santy?' Why you do that?"

"Because you usually know. Now, what time is it?"

Santy pulled on his black pants and fastened his belt. "My stomach tells me it is time to eat." He peered through the shades at the Memphis skyline. "What kind of breakfast you think is free?"

"Okay, okay," Eduardo said. "I'm coming. I might as well be with Arturo, you so bossy today, eh?"

At the mention of Arturo, Santy's body stiffened. "We will not speak of Arturo. We must find Kimmy Cruz."

"*Sí*. Or Arturo will find us." The room felt as cold as the blade of the knife in Eduardo's backpocket. "Let's go out and find some breakfast, Santy. A man always thinks better with a full stomach."

Santy nodded, but he didn't agree, not completely. Hunger, in the right situations, kept a man alert, ready, and hungry. That was the way he felt right now. A piece of paper slid under the door and Santy reached for it.

"It is jus a bill," Eduardo said. "Forget it, Santy. I already give them the cash."

But, Santy stared at the paper, intrigued. "What is occupancy tax?"

"You ask too many questions. Put that in the trash." He grabbed the paper from Santy's hands and crunched it into a ball. "Now, we will go find something to eat. Arturo called again. He say he is coming to find the Kimmy himself."

Santy shrugged and glimpsed through a crack in the sagging drapes. They reeked of cigarette smoke, despite the no-smoking status of the room. He frowned and rose to peer into the sunlight. "The gringo, he is going back."

"Who? Who is back? Back to where?" Eduardo joined Santy where he stood at the window. He squinted and shook his head in agreement. "Sí, you are correct. It looks jus' like Jupiter Ron."

"*Sí!* Señor Jupiter. He always say to me, 'Call me Jupe.'" Santy grabbed his head as if it throbbed. "I call him nothing."

"He is your customer?"

"*Sí.* But Eduardo, think. Who is his customer, eh? That is the reason he is here."

"Maybe he is looking for you. Or another customer. It is possible."

"But, we saw him...let me see...jus' last week."

"So? Maybe he needs a contact. Go fine out, Santy. Wait, you want me to go with you?"

"No." Santy patted the Colt .38 Super in the waistband of his pants. "I have enough company already. And you have to pick up Arturo at airport, *sí*? I can handle this alone."

Eduardo nodded. "Hokay. But remember, Santy. If he is Jupiter Ron, maybe he know where to fine the Kimmy."

"An if he doesn't know? Maybe he know, but won't help us?"

Eduardo laughed, a deep, sinister chuckle. "If he is Jupiter Ron, he will not be so stupid. And, if he is not him, what is he to us, eh?" He cast his gaze upon the .38 Super. "The bullet, she is fast and cheap."

"Fast and cheap. My favorite kind," Santy said. He turned the knob on the door slowly, carefully. "I'll be back when I'm finished." He opened the door and shut it behind him.

The phone rang just after he left. Eduardo stared at it for a second and sighed. He would have to talk to Arturo. He grabbed the receiver and held it to his ear. "*Hola!*"

The caller hung up on the other end of the line.

He banged the receiver back into the cradle and rushed to the window. Santy and Ron stood beside the magnolia bushes, all of them sweating in the humid heat. Funny thing, Eduardo thought. Alone in the motel room, watching the two men barter the daily deal, he too sweated in the humid heat. The Scotland Yard Inn was like that.

And then, Eduardo spotted her. The woman sauntered to the silver Caddy in a way that looked too, well...so familiar. Still, he couldn't place her. With a scarf wrapped tightly around her hair, he could barely guess her haircolor. He would guess blonde, oh, for the heck of it. A guy could dream, couldn't he? Looked to him like this woman tried them all, sooner or later...

"Hey, Shelby!" Jupe said. Eduardo didn't recognize the new name. *Must be one of Jupe's customers.* Still, from where he stood, this Shelby was the exact image of Kimmy Cruz. Everything was the same, except for the fact that Kimmy had blonde, very blonde hair in comparison to Shelby's hair, now a vibrant shade of red. Even the way she strutted to the Caddy, a little brisker pace now—she didn't stop to acknowledge Jupe's greeting or presence—reminded him of Kimmy. That behavior, that deliberate snub, right there—that was Kimmy Cruz all over again. Eduardo never thought he would meet another woman as rude as Kimmy. To be so rude was an epidemic, it seemed, it...

Wait a minute. Eduardo saw the panic in the woman's eyes.

Like ants beneath an elephant's foot, the Caddy's monstrous tires flattened the beer cans. With Shelby behind the wheel, the Caddy roared out of the parking lot. Santy and Jupe leapt into Jupe's Dodge Charger, tires screeching like a siren at midnight. In Eduardo's mind, this redhead resembled someone they all knew. Perhaps, Santy and Jupe found the missing girl. They could find her, but they couldn't make Eduardo or anyone else, demonstrate mercy or understanding. The Kimmy would have to beg for those things herself.

Eduardo admired the magnolias, glistening in the Memphis sun. That was for the flowers to do; Eduardo liked to keep things cool.

Like Arturo.

Twenty Three

"We might as well go on," Cobra said. "Shelby, or whoever she really is, isn't coming back this way. Not today anyway." He sucked a final drag from the nub of a cigarette and stubbed it out with the sole of his sneaker. "I could go for some pancakes. How about you, Suggs. Suggs? What are you looking at?"

"He's not looking at anything," Di said. "El, what's wrong?"

Elvin stared at the gravel road that led to Shelby's trailer. He didn't blink or, for that matter, seem to hear anything they said. "I thought she'd be here by now."

"Does she know you're here?"

"Well, she ought to know."

"Suggs, there's something I need to get off my chest," Cobra said.

"If it's that you don't think she's the one for me, then save it. Because she is. I know it. I knew it from the time I laid eyes on her 'lil face. There is nothing you can say that will change my mind."

Cobra glanced at Di. She nodded and mouthed the words, "Go on."

"Well, I have to say this because if you hadn't picked me up when you did, I plain woulda frozen to death. I owe you one big one, at least."

"Where are you going with this?"

"While you and Di were talking memories back in the bedroom at your house, your lady love was asking me a big favor. One which I refused, by the way."

"Now, I don't own her, so…"

"I'm not talking about that kind of favor, Suggs." He paused. "Man, I need a cigarette for this one. And a glassful of Jack."

"What the hell did she ask you to do? Join the Marines?"

"Very funny. It's something just about as crazy—at least for a guy like me."

"El," Di said, "Shelby is in a lot of trouble."

"So, you two want me to leave her there? Is that it?"

"No Suggs, but we think you should know the truth."

"The truth is, she's got two Mexican guys, pretty rough ones, chasing her all over the country. According to her, they think she killed somebody's brother and stole some money from them."

Elvin began to laugh. "Do you hear yourself, Cobra? You need to sleep some is all. You're hallucinating. Forget it. 'Sides, why would she tell you all of this?"

"She's afraid they'll catch up with her and kill her before she can shake them. So, she wanted me to go after them. Somebody that looked a lot like you told her I liked to shoot people."

"Well, don't you?"

"I know how to do it and I'm good at it. That's the way folks are, Suggs. They like to do what they're good at. So do I. All of which does not make me a bad person."

"What's your point, buddy?"

"My point is this, Suggs. You and your angel need to have a heart to heart about who she really is, and what she's doing here. Because I don't think you know her whole story—not by a long shot. No pun intended."

"And you know what?" Elvin leaned forward until their noses touched. "She doesn't know the whole story about me and Cherie neither. She didn't ask anything and I didn't volunteer. Know why? Because it wasn't the right time." He backed away and stood by the edge of the trailer. "I figure our stories will come out a little at a time, when we're ready to handle the truth. I mean, mine isn't exactly a fairy tale, either. Remember the two guys who came after my wife?

Remember the Hubble brothers?"

"Who could forget Arnold Hubble?" Di said. "I never saw anyone who could eat 24/7 before I met up with him. And those potato chip and mayonnaise sandwiches he liked to carry around in waxed paper were disgusting."

"My favorite derelict was Walter," Cobra said. "That was one mean dude. Can't say I ever enjoyed shooting anybody as much as I did the day I nailed Walter and his slob of a brother. As far as I'm concerned, the world was a better place without those two *hombres*."

Elvin looked triumphant. "Y'all see my point. Nobody's perfect, but Shelby's about as close as she can get, far as I can tell. Perfect for me. I'm willing to plain overlook what doesn't matter. Especially if she's willing to do the same."

"Okay, El," Di said. "We heard you. Right, Cobra? Cobra?"

Cobra didn't seem to hear a word Di said. The orange Dodge Charger that pulled into the gravel lot captured his concentration; the two amigos, especially the one who spoke something that sounded suspiciously like Spanish, fascinated him. His hand reached into the waistband of his jeans. His fingers gripped the butt of the Glock pistol.

Elvin didn't say a word. He thought he saw the glint of a silver Caddy rounding a bend in the road that approached the trailer park. The car belonged to him. Shore 'nuf. But…

"Spread out," Cobra said. "There's three of them."

"There's just two in the Charger now, Cobra," Elvin said. "Who's driving my car?"

Di peered into the shadows and covered her face with her hands as if her head hurt. "Tell him, Cobra."

"Suggs," he said, "it's Shelby. You'd better let Di and me handle this."

"You're wrong, you…"

A streak of white and gold darted between the trailers. "What was Shelby wearing the last time you saw her, El?" Di whispered.

"Pair of white jeans, with big gold buttons on the… Listen, y'all, I think…"

A bullet popped somewhere between the trailers.

"That was close," Cobra said. "I'm gonna move up. Di, cover me." He flattened his body against a nearby trailer and took a deep breath. At the sound of the bullet, the panic and anxiety flooded his senses. *Not now. No time for that. Not now.*

Di pulled the Browning Hi–Power out of her purse. Elvin faded back into the shadows between the trailers.

Gilda crept from her trailer to investigate the noise. The man came from behind. The gun rammed into her back before she could turn to face him. Santy grinned, and the crimson eyes of a demon glowed in the shadows. "*Buenos dias, Señora.*" The gun jammed between Gilda's shoulder blades. "Where is the Kimmy, eh? Jus tell me, that's all ju haf to do, *Señora.* I will count to—lemme see—five. One, two, *tres, quattro...*"

"Here, Pancho!" Cobra's voice whispered from behind a trailer. "She's over here. You're a fool to bother an old lady. She doesn't know anything."

"Who is that, eh?" Santy said.

From the shadows of another trailer, Di emerged. "I know where she is, Jorge."

"Who is Jorge?"

"That's you, isn't it? Don't tell me your name isn't Jorge. Oh, my. There I go again, telling secrets I shouldn't tell."

Cobra's arm jutted from behind the trailer across the road, gripping the neck of Jupe's shirt. "Look what I found. You know this guy, Pancho?"

"Let him go! Let him go, or I shoot the *Señora.*"

"Nossir, I don't b'lieve you will," Elvin said.

Two shots exploded, one to the heart, followed by one to the head. Santy dropped in a heap.

Elvin stood in at the corner of Gilda's trailer, with his Colt Commander poised in his right hand. He winked at the terrified woman, still trembling from the shock. "I hate showoffs, don't you?"

"Oh man, are you guys in trouble now," Jupe said. "You have no idea what just happened here." His skin looked a putrid shade of green.

"That's what you're for," Cobra said. "You're gonna tell us all about it."

"I'm going to go knock on Shelby's trailer," Elvin said. "Find out what this is all about."

"Elvin, for once, don't do the first thing that pops into your head," Di said.

"Hey, man," Jupe said, "I'm here to tell you. I don't know her, but she's right."

Sirens whined in the distance, and the blare intensified with each passing second. The flash of red and blue lights illuminated the narrow lanes in the trailer park.

"Who's that?" Elvin said.

"That's the sheriff. Someone must have called him."

"Don't look at me," Jupe said.

"They're going to want to talk to me," Elvin said. "Probably take my gun for evidence, me being from out of state now and all."

"Step into my place for a minute," Gilda said.

Elvin followed her into the neat living room. She pulled the old Colt revolver from between the cushions of the sofa. "Here." She placed it in his hands. "After what you did for me, I want you to have this. Something tells me you're going to need it before all of this is over."

"I can't accept this, Mrs. Shultz. It's your family treasure. One of them should have it."

"They're all gone but me. And, if it hadn't been for you, I would have been too. Please, make an old woman happy, you big hunk." Gilda glanced at the revolver in Elvin's strong hands. "It looks better in your hands anyway."

Elvin stared at the pistol with reverence in his eyes. "Can't tell you how honored I am to have a gun that belonged to your daddy." He thumbed the hammer back to half cocked position and checked the cylinder. Five fat .45 Colt cartridges gleamed in the light. He pulled the hammer to full cock and let it down on the empty chamber. "Thanks," he said.

"Elvin!" Di's voice sounded urgent. "There's a sheriff out here wanting to talk to you."

Elvin smiled and hugged Gilda. "Seems I have an audience waiting on me, ma'am. Better get to it before it gets to me. I'll come back and get this after I talk to the sheriff." He winked at Gilda and hustled out of the front door.

"If only I was just a few years younger," Gilda murmured. "What a man!" For a moment, she recalled how she turned heads, once upon a time, dressed in her heels and pearls. *Would a man like Elvin looked at her twice?* She chose to believe he would. Tonight, that was enough for her.

Twenty Four

"I've been looking for Jupiter for months," the man said. His face looked like it was covered in tanned cowhide. Elvin noticed his hands, calloused and large for his small build. "And, I come to Memphis and find him, keeping company with the likes of Santy Corejo. I can't believe it." He lit a cigarette and blew a puff of smoke into the steamy haze. "Where's my manners? I apologize. The name's Gomez. Gary Gomez. I'm the sheriff around here now, but I spent enough time in Texas to know what those two names mean."

Elvin shielded his eyes with his hands to block the sun. "You know that much about the Mexican guys?"

"Hell, yes. I'm from Texas, originally. Everybody around El Paso knows about Corejo. What I'm wondering is, where's his Boss man?"

"His who?"

"Corejo usually keeps company with a dude named Ruiz. Eduardo Ruiz. That is one rough, very mean character. Avoid him at all costs. If he hears someone shot Corejo, he'll be looking for the person who did it, and if he's got a car, he'll get here tonight. My guess is, he's got one—and, he will be."

"Well, I'll stay out of dark alleys for awhile, how's that? Right now, I'm going to check on Shelby. I need to see if she's alright, with all this commotion around and all." He hustled up the steps that led to Shelby's trailer, knocked on the door, and waited. And waited some more. He knocked again—and waited, until Gilda opened her door.

"Elvin! I thought you'd gone by now. Step on in here and get what my daddy left you. Shelby's gone, baby. Tonight's her opening night at the Heartbreak Hideway." She frowned. "Didn't she tell you? Oh, I'll bet she was just nervous, that's all. Didn't want to jinx the first night."

"Sakes alive! She got that job after all!" Elvin strode out the door and down the steps, over to Di and Cobra. "C'mon, we're going over to Beale Street for a show."

"What kind of a show?" Di said. "Am I dressed for it?"

"You worry about the craziest stuff sometimes," Cobra said. "Ain't gonna see me worrying about wearing the right clothes to a show on Beale Street."

Elvin scanned Cobra's ensemble, such as it was. "You might want to fix that ketchup stain on the front of that T-shirt, buddy."

"It's barbecue sauce, Suggs."

"Why didn't you say so? Just leave it, then. They serve barbeque stuff where we're going, so you'll fit right in."

Di considered the pair before her. "I wouldn't go hog wild, El. You mean, if he gets in, they won't throw him out."

The redhead laughed, a hearty laugh that Elvin hadn't heard in a long time. "Any place called the Heartbreak Hideaway might let anyone in and throw anybody out."

"Sounds like we're headed for the right place. Let's go, Suggs."

Memphis Airport parking lot, late afternoon

"Arturo!" Eduardo hugged the corpulent man and kissed him on both cheeks. "It is good to see you looking so well. Welcome!"

Arturo's black eyes scanned the landscape like a spotlight. "It is very green, this Memphis, Tennessee. And very hot, eh? Like Mexico."

"*Sí.*"

"Where is Santy?"

"I don't know. He doesn't answer his phone calls." Eduardo punched the button to speed dial Santy's phone. It rang and rang, but no one answered.

Arturo shook his massive head. It reminded Eduardo of a bull.

"America. No respect they have for nothing. Santy has been here what, two, three days and nights? And he lost his courtesy?"

Eduardo stabbed the air with his index finger. "Las' time I see Santy, he was with Jupiter Ron!"

"Jupiter? Who is Jupiter Ron?"

"He is our contact. From St. Francis House, in Texas. Long time ago, but a favor cannot forget a favor, *sí*?"

"Eduardo, you try my patience."

"Jupiter and Santy go to the El Dorado to get the Kimmy."

"Now, Santy, he no return my calls." In a furious burst of energy, he punched the buttons on his cell phone. "Jupe? Is that you? Jupe, why you not call?" His face grew pale, and his voice dropped to a whisper. Eduardo's shoulders slumped and a tear dripped from the corner of his eye. "*Ya chapo faros y se fue el cielo.*"

"What?" Arturo's face was covered with beads of sweat. "Where is Santy?"

Eduardo glanced to the clouds. "He has smoked his last *Faro*. He is now in heaven."

"What do you mean?" Arturo pounded the dashboard of the Mercury.

"Jupiter Ron, he say someone shot Santy at the El Dorado Trailer Court. He is dead. The Sheriff Gomez, he has Jupiter Ron with him."

Arturo trembled with fury. "Who is responsible for this atrocity?"

"The Kimmy, of course. But, it was a man that shot Santy. Jupiter Ron says it was a boyfriend."

"I'll kill them both." Arturo stroked the Colt Python in his shoulder holster. "I'll enjoy it. This one is mine, Eduardo. Take me to where they are."

Eduardo blinked and stared at the crowd on Beale Street. "We are here, Arturo. Thees is where we foun them before."

"You must be kidding."

"I am not."

Arturo's face melted into a smile. "Look." He pointed to a banner stretched across the front of the Heartbreak Hideaway: *Krystal Light Debut Tonight!* "Maybe we know Krystal Light, eh Ruiz?"

"Jupiter Ron thinks we do."

Arturo stroked his gun. His jaw stiffened. "Yes. I think we do too. The question is, does she have the boyfriend, the one with a gun? That is the question, Eduardo."

"Jupiter Ron wants us to pay his bail, Arturo. He says he can help us."

"Do we trust him?"

"Not completely."

"Then, I will think about it. I have lost enough already. Save your cash for tips, *comprende*?" Arturo frowned and stared at the storefront display in *Arlo's Free Advice*, next to the Heartbreak Hideaway. What is that in the shop window?"

Eduardo eased out of the driver's seat and headed over to the plate glass window. "It looks like a seat for the toilet. But wait! When you close it, you see the face of the Elvis Presley. Very beautiful. You like, Arturo? The sign says it glows in the dark. Only $450 U.S. dollars."

"A treasure, to be sure. But first, let us do our business. And then, we will buy our souvenir. I want to have something special to remember this trip." He laughed, and the forked-tongue of a snake rattled and spit. "The perfect epitaph for the Kimmy."

Backstage, the Heartbreak Hideaway

Shelby fluffed her hair and took a deep breath before her first venture onto the smoky stage. She wished she hadn't agreed to perform tonight. She almost, just almost, called Lurlene and cancelled her "debut." The truth was, she wanted to sing a song she wrote herself, and tonight seemed like the perfect time. For a moment, she indulged in the luxury of a diversion, and thought about Elvin Suggs.

He was the kind of a man she thought she would never meet. All of these years, she deceived and yes, consoled herself with the belief that a man like him didn't exist. If she allowed herself to stay much longer, she wouldn't be able to leave. That knowledge scared her so much she knew she couldn't stay. Elvin Suggs was genuine, the real deal. He deserved a better future than her desperate dreams could promise him.

Shelby knew her life depended on running. She didn't like to admit it, but she ran often and well. When a person does anything often enough, a behavior becomes second nature. This is true, even if the person doesn't particularly like whatever it is they're doing so often. They may need to do it more often than they like, even when they don't particularly like it, to make up for the natural talent they don't have. Shelby had been running all of her life. By now, she did it very, very well.

After she collected her pay tonight, Jupe would pick her up and she'd start running again, just like the night she left Myles.

There was no point in running from Jupe anymore. Like it or not, he was her soulmate. Some things she could alter to fit a situation— and, she had done that when she could, just to survive. But, Shelby also knew that in this life, a person had to accept the things they couldn't change. She tried to recall a prayer she once heard at a funeral; something about knowing the difference between what things could be changed and what things couldn't. She couldn't recall the exact words, but it didn't matter anyway. She stopped praying a long time ago, more than twenty years now. What was the point in praying, when it seemed to her like no one listened except her own self? She decided it wasn't healthy to talk to herself. So, she stopped.

Only problem now was, Jupe hadn't called when he said he would. That was not Jupe's style. He could be arrogant, stubborn and selfish, but he was not unreliable. Shelby knew of only a few reasons that Jupe would cancel his appointment with her. *Wait a minute…*Jupe never cancelled any appointment with her. What happened to Jupe?

Rusty just finished his last bad joke, out there on the stage. Maybe when the place started to turn a few bucks, he and Lurlene could hire a warm-up act. "And now, our new sensation, here all the way from Reno, let's hear it for Krystal Light!"

Her heart thumped so strongly, it felt like it might burst. *How did Rusty Tate know she used to work in Reno?* She strummed the first few bars of *The Wrong Side of Memphis* and tried her best to work the audience, connect with their mood. That's when she saw Elvin.

His smile unnerved her, but she maintained her composure. There was something about that man that was so engaging, she felt like she had known him all of her life. Even better, she felt like there was nothing she could tell him that would drive him away or make him leave. No matter what she told him, he understood what she did and why she did it. Elvin Suggs was first-class. She didn't deserve him, and certainly, he didn't deserve her. She decided she just couldn't ask a man like him to accept the ghosts of her past; and so, she would have to leave.

A man like Elvin didn't need a woman like Kimmy Cruz or Krystal Light in his life. She stopped being Shelby Swain such a long time ago that she couldn't remember when she left. Besides, she knew Shelby was never coming back. She had crossed a line that couldn't be retraced. Maybe it was sometime around the time when she left Myles and went to Chicago with Jupe, but it had been coming for a while. No matter how she viewed her dilemma, the conclusion never changed. Elvin Suggs deserved better.

"Thank you for that big Tennessee welcome!" Shelby said. The place was packed. The beer flowed like a creek in a thunderstorm. "I'd like to thank the folks at the Heartbreak Hideaway for the chance to sing here this evening. And, there is one special person in the audience tonight who also deserves a big thank you. My next song is dedicated to the first person to welcome me back home, Mr. Elvin Suggs. I wrote it myself, and it's called *"Why Should I?"*

Elvin stared with rapt admiration while Shelby crooned the poignant lyrics. *Why should I cry, when I know I, can't stop from thinking bout you even though I, know that we're through, no me and you, why should I?* For a fleeting moment, Shelby felt that maybe she should stay; maybe she could change.

She knew better. The last time she decided to change, she ended up in Tijuana. She was still waiting for the payback on that macabre makeover.

Patter the rain, I can't explain. Why should I? She finished the song and strolled off of the stage. Her show ended to a roar of applause.

They were waiting behind the steps.

Twenty Five

Elvin leapt to his feet. From beneath his seat, he yanked a small bouquet of wildflowers.

"Elvin, you shouldn't have!" Di said. Her face brightened at the sight of the rich hues of the autumn blossoms.

"Ain't they grand? Just a little something I grabbed at the Piggly Wiggly grocery store on the way. Wanted something special for Shelby's first show, you know. I'm going backstage to give these. I won't be long."

Cobra waited until Elvin disappeared to speak. "Elvin, you shouldn't have!" he said, his hand on his hip. "Did you really want flowers from the Piggly Wiggly store? Money'd be better spent on a pack of smokes."

"You don't understand."

"I understand you're disappointed in something. What, I don't know. It can't be that bunch of weeds he's fixin' to give to the angel."

"Doesn't Valerie ever get her feelings hurt?"

"Oh, yeah. And when she does, you know exactly who, why and wherefore. Oh, and you better duck when she reaches to throw a bottle of ketchup or beer at your head— sometimes, it's a can of that nasty hairspray—and let me tell you what, that stuff hurts."

"That's terrible."

"That's Valerie. Take it or leave it. But, it's real and it ain't going to change for nobody, especially me. But, I always know where I stand. And, I like it that way. This one that Suggs has going here, this Shelby... now, she would drive me crazy in under a half an hour."

"Just like Cherie did."

"You know something? You are absolutely right. You'd think Suggs would get tired of a woman like that, wouldn't you?"

Di stared at the stage where just moments earlier, Shelby had performed a song written especially for Elvin.

"Anymore," she said, "I don't know what to think."

Cobra's jaw dropped. "I'll tell you what I think. That Shelby's some kind of woman."

Backstage

Shelby wished she had a flashlight. She could barely see two feet in front of her. She startled at a rustling sound, and glanced toward the steps. She saw nothing.

"Shhh, Eduardo," Arturo said, "we don't want company."

Eduardo flashed the knife, *el cuchillo*, and grinned. Shrouded in the shadows, the blade glinted like a diamond ring on a new bride's finger. He didn't speak. He concentrated on his prey, now rounding the corner. It was time.

He never saw him coming.

Elvin turned the corner behind Shelby, just in time to see the bright glint of steel beneath the lights. "Oh no, you don't." He grasped Eduardo's right arm at the elbow and straightened it, just before he pulled it up and snapped it like a breadstick.

Shelby screamed at the sight of the Latin *diablos,* and did what she did best. She ran.

"Aghhhhh!" Eduardo wailed and dropped to the ground.

Arturo glared at Elvin. "So you are the boyfriend with the gun, eh? The man who shot Santos Corejo? Answer me, gringo!" He reached inside his coat and Elvin saw it—the .357 caliber Colt Python.

"You'll *need* this before it's over." Even as the time seemed to slow, Gilda's words echoed in his head. Elvin snatched the Single Action Army revolver from his waistband.

Arturo's finger was on the trigger when Elvin fired. A crimson stain blossomed on his forehead. With a soft moan, he slumped in a heap behind Eduardo.

"You killed him!" Eduardo said.

Elvin recocked the hammer on the old Colt and covered the body with his jacket. "Don't give me any more ideas, friend."

Cobra was the first to appear, followed by Di.

"Elvin, are you okay?" she said. "Where's Shelby? Who are these guys?"

"What I want to know is, who let these guys in?" Elvin said. "They tried to murder Shelby."

"You will be very sorry," Eduardo said. "Arturo, he have many more brothers."

Rusty hustled down the hall and stopped at the sight of the gathering crowd. "Oh no! Lurlene! We didn't need a mess like this. Lurlene! Call the police! Call an ambulance."

Elvin handed his revolver to Cobra. "Cover this hombre for me while I check on Shelby."

Cobra grabbed the revolver and nodded. His eyes never wavered from Eduardo's face.

Rusty watched Elvin twist the knob to the door of Shelby's dressing room. "Hey, that's a private place. What do you want in there?" He poked his head inside the stuffy room. "Okay, who opened that little winda?"

Elvin didn't hear him. The open window above the white porcelain sink meant nothing to him. His broken heart lay in the pink clutch purse on the wooden dressing table, beating to a rhythm only he could hear. That pink purse used to ride in the glovebox of his Caddy. With trembling fingers, he opened it, and found the Missouri driver's license that belonged to a lady named Shelby Lynn Swain. Well, she looked like the woman he loved. Shore 'nuf.

"Listen up, Mr. Suggs. Are you going to keep mooning over a bad picture of a woman you already know? Or are you going to help me with this window?"

Elvin paused for a moment. When he finally spoke, his smile struggled to conceal the pain his eyes revealed. "Mr. Tate, is it? Nossir, I don't believe I know that woman." He bit his lip and took a deep breath. "I thought I did. But, I don't, after all." Suddenly, the smile faded. "Mistakes do happen."

The window slammed. Elvin closed the purse and laid it gently on the dressing table. "I b'lieve I'm finished here."

Days later...
The Grapevine Detective Agency
St. Louis, Missouri

"Y'all don't have to tiptoe around me, you know." Elvin leaned back in the recliner and punched buttons into the television remote. "I'm doing just dandy. I'm okay. I really am."

"We know that, Suggs," Cobra said. "It's just that..."

"What?"

"These nachos you made, well..." He licked his fingers and strolled into the kitchen.

Di touched Elvin on the shoulder. "It's okay, El. You just forgot to add the chips before you piled on all of the other stuff."

Cobra strode into the room with a bag of corn chips and snapped the cellophane to open the wrapper. He poured the contents onto the plate. "I'll just move things around a little bit and... *Voila!*" he said. In one stroke, he swept the chips under the mountain of melted cheese, jalapeno peppers, barbeque sauce and sour cream.

Elvin turned to assess the piled food from a different angle. "You know, that looks danged good, Cobra. We should work together more often."

Di covered her head with her hands. "What do you call that, uh...creation?"

Cobra turned to Elvin. "Suggs? What do we call that?"

Elvin grinned at Di. "How about the Second Chance?"

Cobra lifted a glass of Jim Beam in a toast. "To my friend, Suggs, and the Second Chance." He glanced at Di over the rim of the glass. She was getting ready to bring up the blonde; he could hear the rumble of the thunder in the distance. Speaking of chances...

"Hey, it's *Jeopardy!*" Elvin said. "I just love that show, don't you? It's so educational. I mean, don't you feel like you always learn something after you watch it?"

One glance at the frown on Di's face convinced Cobra of at least one thing. He never loved that show as much as he did right now.

"Sure, Suggs."

"Elvin," Di said, "I've been meaning to talk to you about—"

"Di," Cobra said, "can't you see Suggs is watching *Jeopardy*? Let the man concentrate."

Cobra felt the burn in her stare, and focused on the screen. A shiver ran down his arms like a bucket full of cold rainwater.

"Look Cobra, it's the Big One," Elvin said. "Sakes alive! They're playing for the *Jeopardy* Championship. Those are the big money prizes! Cherie used to love to watch the *Jeopardy Championship Show.*"

"I'll bet she did," Di said. "Elvin, whatever happened to—"

Elvin leaned forward in his chair. "Hey y'all, I know that guy! Can't place the face, you know, but I know that guy from somewhere. Cobra, take a look. Do you know him?"

Cobra studied the wiry man with the wavy auburn hair. He shook his head. "Can't imagine who that might be." Cobra helped himself to a helping of chips, coated with barbecue sauce and cheese. The wiry man grinned broadly into the television camera and waved to his fans.

"I do believe I never saw a happier guy," Elvin said. "Hey Di, maybe you ought to go on that show. Then, you could be happy like him."

"Here it comes, the $50,000 question," Cobra said.

"I have a $50,000 question," Di said. "Elvin, why won't you—"

"For the *Jeopardy* Championship," the announcer said, "the answer is, 'The River City famous for duck parades and dog races.' What is the question? You have 30 seconds."

"Whoo-eee," Elvin said. "Talk about pressure. Dogs and ducks, dogs and ducks." He glanced at Vanna, lying beside his recliner. "Gal, do you know anything about ducks and races?"

"Mr. Arseneaux? Your answer, please?"

"Arsen-what?" Elvin said. "Sounds familiar. I would have remembered a name like that, shore 'nuf."

Beads of sweat glistened on the contestant's lined forehead. His lips pursed together, Cobra wondered if he might be unable to answer the question; or rather, provide the question to the answer.

"Okay," Nester said, "here's my best shot." He closed his eyes. "What is…Memphis?" He opened one eye and stared as if he had seen a ghost.

"You're absolutely right! *Jeopardy* fans, we have a champion!" He passed the microphone to Nester. "Tell us, Mr. Arseneaux, what will you do with your prize money?"

"Look y'all, Mr. Arsen looks like he's crying," Elvin said.

"It's Arseneaux, Elvin. His name is Arseneaux." Di said.

Nester choked back his tears. "I want to thank you for letting me be on the show. This money is my second chance, and I couldn't be any happier to have it. But, you know, I just realized something." He stopped and smiled into the camera. "What the most important thing to me about being a *Jeopardy* contestant was the chance to be on the show—not whether or not I won the money. Don't get me wrong, I *will* enjoy the money. But, I want to donate some of it back to help the military vets out there, especially ones like me who watch this great show." Again, Nester smiled for the camera. "Remember, pass it on."

"Our new *Jeopardy* Champion, ladies and gentlemen, Nester P. Arseneaux! Let's give him another big round of applause."

"I knew I knew that guy from somewhere." Elvin patted Vanna's head. "He was in 'Nam."

Cobra frowned at the suggestion. "I don't recall anyone by that name, Suggs. And that's a name I would remember. Di, how about you?"

"Nope."

Elvin snapped his fingers. "I know! I picked him up one day, and gave him a ride."

"Suggs, that's good enough for now," Cobra said. "We believe you, don't we, Di?"

"Elvin, after all that's happened, I hope you stop picking up people you don't know."

Elvin shook his head. "Never going to stop doing that, Di. I like the way Nester said he didn't care if he won or lost, as long as he got a chance to try." Elvin's voice cracked with emotion. "You might feel like I lost something, picking up a girl like Shelby and letting myself fall in love again, just a little bit. But, let me tell you something. A girl like Shelby gave me the chance to try again. It doesn't matter if I won or lost. I'm back in the game again. And it feels mighty good." Elvin stared at Vanna. "She almost looks like she's smiling, don't she?"

"Sure, Suggs," Cobra said. "We all are. We're just glad you're back."

"Me too." Elvin grinned. "Pass it on!"

THE END

Also by Claire Applewhite

The Wrong Side of Memphis
St. Louis Hustle
Candy Cadillac
Crazy For You
Voices of Excellence™

Reviews for Claire's other books

About *The Wrong Side of Memphis:*

"Get ready to meet some of the most intriguing characters ever. There are secrets and surprises galore to be found among the tenants of the Jewel Arms Apartments—and Claire Applewhite brings them all to life in *The Wrong Side of Memphis.*"
—Tess Gerritsen, author of *The Keepsake*

"This is an old-fashioned who-dunnit, and don't let the title fool you. It's set in St. Louis, a hard-scrabble apartment building where all the tenants have dreams and secrets, and some have motive and opportunity. It's a place I might not want to live, but I sure enjoyed my visit."
—Bill McClellan, St. Louis Post-Dispatch

An entertaining, atmospheric read.
—Kirkus Reviews

About *St Louis Hustle:*

"Author Applewhite has created an engrossing tale that presents the setting almost as one of the cast of characters. If you like neatly rendered, nicely plotted fiction, you'll finish *St. Louis Hustle* in one sitting. For those who know little or nothing about St. Louis, Applewhite's novel is the perfect gateway to the Gateway City."
—John Lutz, author of *Mr. X* and *Single White Female*

I loved all the St. Louis landmarks cleverly woven into the story. The characters are well-developed — I seem to know people just like them. An enjoyable read. I recommend you check it out.
—Patt Pickett, author of *The Marriage Whisperer*

"Applewhite isn't afraid to stretch the boundaries of noir fiction..."
—Kirkus Reviews

About *Candy Cadillac:*

"Taut writing, memorable characterization and a superbly evocative setting."
—Kirkus Reviews

About *Crazy For You:*

"Don't even think about putting author Claire Applewhite's writing style into any known category; she simply won't fit. Her writing dazzles and sizzles, but even those words don't nail it. Just when you think you'll put *Crazy For You* down, you find you can't. The characters are so real you find yourself wondering how Applewhite got inside your head, the situations so absurd that only the naked truth of our own lives come close to a parallel. This is a writer bound to make a name for herself, one who can't help but attract a huge, fanatic Applewhite-loving audience."
—Esther Luttrell, author, national speaker, screenwriter

"Claire Applewhite's *Crazy for You* is a delicious story of romantic obsession. A wealthy family's patriarch schemes to replace his aging wife with a beautiful young woman. The son-in-law recently welcomed into the family has a case of love at first sight—but not with his new wife. Fierce passions tug at the characters' hearts as obsession rips through the two marriages.Intrigues collide and unravel as *Crazy for You* builds suspense and takes readers on a roller coaster. A great cast of supporting characters add to the complexity of the plot. A quick read, but one that delves into themes of loyalty, betrayal, and the true meaning of marriage."
—Shirley Kennett, Author, *PJ Gray series*

About *Voices of Excellence:*

"Applewhite's innovative communication program demonstrates the heights that urban youth can reach when the larger community takes a genuine interest. Applewhite recruited adult mentors to aid every step of the way. Her sound basic program in the hands of committed volunteers results in breathtaking success year after year. Any civic-minded group wanting to change lives for the better and rewrite the future of our country for a more harmonious tomorrow would do well to use *Voices of Excellence*™ in their own hometowns."

—MARY D. ROSS, B.A., B.S ED., M. ED., Speech and Theatre Association of Missouri Emeritus, Member of the Hall of Fame of the National Speech and Debate Association

"At the conclusion of the 2011 academic year at Loyola Academy, I attended the Graduation Mass. The
8th graders offered petitions at the Offertory. I noticed they were very hard to understand. Mrs. Claire Applewhite was developing *Voices of Excellence*™ at that time, and we discussed the possibility of working with the 6th, 7th, & 8th grade boys, at Loyola! The improvement in 2012, after the introduction of VOE, was stunning! We continue to streamline the program, to fit their curriculum."

—ANGELA ZYLKA, St. Louis Metropolitan Medical Society Alliance

As judges for the students' presentations, we were impressed by the progress each grade made in developing a coherent and lucid essay and also learning how to present it before an audience in such a short period (since this is a summer program). These young men (as Loyola calls them, not boys) came from disadvantaged environments, often with very poor formal English writing skills and virtually no knowledge of how to present their ideas in a public forum. From that, within a few weeks, through this program, the young participants learned the prerequisites for honing their ideas and sharing them with others. These newly formed abilities were topped off by the speech contest, which gave them a chance to excel and "win" through their ideas, writings, and presentation skills. For most, if not all, a new experience.

The *Voices of Excellence* program stands as a model for developing skills in writing and oratory. Through these skills, it encourages the young participants to have a sense of pride and achievement in their own intellectual abilities and prepares them for their future in a participatory democracy.

—Pamela A DeVoe, PhD
—Ronald E Mertz, PhD

Claire Applewhite Bio

Claire Applewhite, a mystery and romantic suspense author, is a graduate of St. Louis University. Her published books include *The Wrong Side of Memphis, Crazy For You, St. Louis Hustle, Candy Cadillac, Tennessee Plates and Voices of Excellence*. She is an adjunct professor at the University of Missouri St. Louis, and has served as a Past President of the Missouri Writers Guild and Board member of the Midwest Chapter, Mystery Writers of America. Her organizational memberships include the St. Louis Metropolitan Press Club, St. Louis Writers Guild, Sisters in Crime, Ozark Writers League and Mystery Writers of America.